THE

Mrs. Meade Mysteries

Vol. 1.

THE

Mrs. Meade

Mysteries

VOL. I

ELISABETH GRACE FOLEY

Published 2014 by Second Sentence Press

Cover design by Historical Editorial
Silhouette artwork by Casey Koester

ISBN: 1495463680
ISBN-13: 978-1495463686

TABLE OF CONTENTS

THE

SILVER SHAWL

Gloucester: In my opinion thou seest not well.
Simpcox: Yea, master, clear as day, I thank God and Saint Alban.
Gloucester: Say'st thou me so? What color is this cloak of?

~ *William Shakespeare*

Mrs. Henney knocked lightly at the door. The early morning sunlight was streaming in through the potted plants in the window at the end of the hall, over the faded strip of carpet down the middle of the floor, and gleaming on the polished wood of the door by which Mrs. Henney stood. Having waited with lifted hand, but received no answer, she knocked again.

"Miss Charity?" she said. "Breakfast is ready."

She listened with her head tilted toward the door, but there was no sound. Mrs. Henney smiled indulgently to herself and turned away. Sleeping a little late, she didn't doubt—Miss Charity'd been that busy these last few weeks, and down to Miss Lewis's last evening as usual. No harm in letting her get a bit of rest, Mrs. Henney thought as she descended the back stairs to the kitchen—she would take a tray up to Miss Charity's room after she had served breakfast to her other ladies and gentlemen.

(There was, strictly speaking, only one elderly gentleman among Mrs. Henney's boarders, but Mrs. Henney always pluralized him when she referred to them as a group. It made her little establishment sound so much more flourishing.)

Breakfast was over, and Mrs. Henney had just finished clearing away the dishes from the dining-room to the kitchen, when the front door banged smartly and Randall Morris took the main stairs to the upstairs hall two at a time, whistling merrily, his quirt swinging from his left hand. He stopped at the same hall door and knocked. "Charity?" he called.

He waited a few seconds, as Mrs. Henney had done, and then knocked again. "Charity, are you there?"

The door across the hall opened and Mrs. Meade looked out. Randall Morris glanced over his shoulder. "'Morning, Mrs. Meade," he said, a friendly smile flashing across his handsome face. "Say, is Charity in? I've got to go over to Jewel Point to see Hart about a yearling, and I just stopped by to see her on the way."

"Good morning, Randall," said Mrs. Meade, smiling pleasantly up at him in return. She was a widow lady of middle age, but one whom age seemed to have softened rather than hardened. Her graying hair still showed hints of the soft brown it had once been, and all the lines of her face were kind. But behind the kindness in her gray-blue eyes there was an expression of quaint humor, as though she knew a good deal more about you than you realized, but was too kind to let you know it.

"Charity hasn't been down this morning," she

said. "Mrs. Henney told us she knocked at her door before breakfast, but she didn't answer. Mrs. Henney supposed she must have been sleeping a little late."

"That's odd," said Randall. He tried the door-knob and found it locked, and knocked once more. "Charity!" he called in a louder voice.

Mrs. Meade had drawn nearer, and they both listened attentively, Randall with his ear close to the door, but neither could hear any sound.

Randall cast an alarmed glance at Mrs. Meade. "You don't think she's ill or something!" he said.

Without waiting for an answer he pounded on the door with his fist in a way that startled all the other boarders in their respective rooms, and then would have immediately forced the door with his shoulder had not Mrs. Meade laid detaining hands on his arm and prudently suggested applying to Mrs. Henney for the spare key.

She performed this office herself, and when she escorted the short and puffing landlady to the top of the stairs Randall was still listening outside the door with a look of strained anxiety.

"I can't hear anything," he said, and the look in his eyes as he thus appealed to Mrs. Meade was almost desperate.

Mrs. Meade put her hand gently on his arm as they watched Mrs. Henney fumble nervously with the keys and at last manage to insert the right one into the lock. The door opened inwards, and Randall pushed unceremoniously past Mrs. Henney into the room. He stopped in the middle of it, looking about him in bewilderment.

The two ladies, who had entered after him in considerable apprehension, likewise looked with astonishment about the room, which was neat, quiet, and empty. The window-shade was drawn halfway down, blocking out most of the morning light and leaving the room mildly dim; the bed was neatly made and had evidently not been slept in.

Randall Morris turned around to stare at the ladies. "Did she go out this morning?" he said.

"Why, no," said Mrs. Henney, whose mouth and eyes were wide. "I was up early as always, and her door was shut when I opened the curtains in the hall. She hasn't come out since."

"But how do you know that? Couldn't she have gone out when you were getting breakfast?"

"Why, no, sir. I can hear every step on those stairs, front or back, when I'm in my kitchen, and nobody went out of the house this morning, not Miss Charity nor anybody."

"Well, then—where is she? When did you see her last?"

"Why, she went out to Miss Lewis's last evening after supper, Mr. Randall, just as usual. I saw her go out then, and I was in bed and asleep before she came back, as I've often been. I let Miss Charity have an outside key so she can come in without waking any-one if it's late and I've already locked up and gone to bed."

"You mean you didn't see her come back last night? or hear her?"

"Why, no, sir."

Mrs. Meade, in the meantime, had with a thoughtful expression crossed the room to the war-drobe and opened it, and stood looking at the simple dresses hanging there. "The dress she wore yesterday is not here," she said. "She was wearing her light green gingham at supper — "

"Yes, I know that dress," blurted Randall fever-ishly, as if that would be some help.

Mrs. Meade lifted a hatbox a few inches from the floor of the wardrobe and shook it gently, and set it down again. "Her summer hat is missing — and her little silk purse, it seems — but everything else appears to be in order. She was wearing that hat when she went out, wasn't she, Mrs. Henney?"

"Yes, yes, that and her shawl. That's what she had on when I saw her go out and — "

Randall interrupted the landlady's trembling recollections, speaking to Mrs. Meade: "Do you mean she didn't come back last night? Then where — "

Mrs. Meade countered the alarm rising in his voice with a calm interruption of her own. "Perhaps she spent the night with Miss Lewis, if their work went very late. Miss Lewis stays at the shop herself some nights if she doesn't feel equal to walking home. You should go and ask her first of all."

"I'll do it," said Randall breathlessly, and plunged out of the room. In a few seconds he was outside untying his horse from Mrs. Henney's gate, and swung up into the saddle. He brought his quirt down sharply across the horse's glossy flank and spurred out of the quiet side street into the main road.

* * *

Sour Springs, Colorado, misnamed by an early settler who did not care for the taste of the mineral water he had found on his land, was a pleasant little mountainside town nestled among the wooded foothills, with pine forests on the crests and lighter green stretches of cultivated farm and ranch land in the valleys between. The snow-crested Rockies all around made a sharp silver and white frame for the dome of clear blue sky arched over it. The sunny main street was a double row of neat frame houses and storefronts punctuated by fenced, tree-shaded side lawns and gardens.

Randall Morris, the son of a Southern family whose fortunes had suffered in the generations following the war, had come West to make his own way in the world several years before. Young, energetic and determined, he was already well on his way to success, breeding and raising horses that bid fair to be as fine as those of Kentucky or Virginia on the slopes of his land at the foot of the mountains. Over the past few months, during his courtship of Charity Bradford, he had spent much of his time building and furnishing a house there. Half Western ranch house, sturdy and square and practical, yet partaking of some of the patrician elegance he remembered from his youth, with its many-paned windows and wide veranda, it gleamed white and pristine among the pines, with wild roses tumbling over themselves in the rocky garden behind it, awaiting its mistress.

Charity was a relative newcomer to Sour Springs, a girl without friends or relatives who had come there seeking work, and had been employed as assistant postmistress at the little post-office that shared a building with the railway depot. Small and dainty, with a sweet voice and rich brown hair, she had a modest, if not quite reserved demeanor, but to those she trusted was capable of a warmth made all the more precious by being hard-won. Randall Morris had fallen tumultuously in love at almost his first sight of her, and immediately devoted his considerable energies to wooing and winning her. Charity had been cautious at first—perhaps as long as it took her to assure herself that his impetuosity was in fact sincerity, though, truth be told, her heart had succumbed almost as soon as his.

Within the year they were engaged, and for the past month Charity had been busy preparing her trousseau, her days passed in a near trance of serene happiness and enlivened by flying visits from her fiancé at all hours of the morning and evening. Randall was a great favorite with the ladies of the boarding-house that had become Charity's home. His manners were both free-and-easy and charming, and he knew how to be attentive to old ladies as well as young ones—though when Charity was present, he was infallibly absorbed in her to the extent that he never saw the knowing nods and smiles and twitters passed among the ladies as they watched the pair. Some of the ladies went so far as to believe they had made the match themselves, but Mrs. Meade, who had a special place in her heart for young people—especially young people in love—knew better.

Randall pulled up his horse in front of a small dry-goods store on the main street and dismounted. The seamstress who was making Charity's dresses rented rooms above the store, and Charity had been visiting her in the evenings for fittings and to assist her in some of the work. With no dowry and little money of her own, Charity had at first been hesitant to accept Randall's insistence on paying for everything himself, but had eventually relented. She had, however, managed to override his expressed opinion that nothing was too good for her, and earnestly endeavored to keep her expenses as modest as possible.

Randall went up the steps to the store and grasped the doorknob, but encountered an unexpected resistance. It was locked. He rattled the door and knocked loudly, and then looking over at the front windows, saw that the shades were drawn. The storekeeper and his family lived at the back of the building, and ordinarily the store was already open for business at this hour. In Randall's disturbed state this was yet another circumstance for alarm. He pounded on the door again. Only silence succeeded.

Randall was looking about him with a confused idea of doing something desperate to attract attention, such as throwing something at an upstairs window, when at last he heard a faint noise. Someone was coming down the stairs inside. The locks of the door scraped as they were turned, and it opened to reveal Diana Lewis, the seamstress.

"I'm sorry," she said, sounding slightly short of breath. "Mr. Benton and his family are out of town until tomorrow, and he asked me to lock up the store at night. I hadn't opened my shop yet this morning."

"Is Charity here?" demanded Randall Morris without preamble.

"Charity?" said Diana Lewis. She sounded surprised. "No, she isn't here."

"What time did she leave last night?"

"She didn't come here last night. I was expecting her, but she never came—I supposed she must have forgotten this once, since she has so much on her mind," said Diana with a slight smile.

"She never came?" said Randall, staring at her unbelievingly.

"No. Why?—is something wrong?"

"She didn't come back to the house last night!

Mrs. Henney says she started out after supper to come here, but—she never came back! Excuse me, Miss Lewis—I've got to—" And turning as he put his hat on he ran blindly down the steps.

* * *

In about the time it takes for a fine horse to travel half a block, Sheriff Andrew Royal was surprised in his office and in the middle of his breakfast by a distraught young man who demanded that Sour Springs be turned upside down and vigorously shaken. Sheriff Royal, once he had got down the half a biscuit with honey which had prevented his interrupting sooner, made routine answer. He told Randall for Pete's sake to calm down, said that yes, he was *aware* that Randall didn't know where Charity was, but it didn't follow that nobody else did, and reached for his hat to lend some credence to his assurances that yes, he'd ask around if anybody'd seen her. As Randall showed signs of giving vent to a burst of outrage at this innocuous understatement, Royal gave him (in an annoyed voice) a list of very good reasons why harm should *not* befall a respectable young woman in a town like Sour Springs, then jammed his hat over his bushy eyebrows and stalked out to prove it.

But by midday, a reasoned anxiety was not only possible, but excusable. After questioning her few closer friends or acquaintances provided no clue to her whereabouts, a general alarm was spread that Charity Bradford was missing, and when it had traveled around the town, the result was that no one had seen her that day.

Royal, once roused, though in no better mood, was persistent. His efforts at length turned up two witnesses. One was a small boy who rightly judged that his being an important witness in the case of a missing young lady would render insignificant the fact that he had been sneaking back into the house at a time he was not supposed to be out of it when he saw her. He had seen Miss Bradford walking along the street after dark, but hadn't gotten close enough to see anything more because he had hidden to avoid her seeing *him*.

The second witness was an old man, rather shaky to begin with, whose closest friends were rather doubtful about his testimony because they knew he was in the habit of taking a nip of something on chilly evenings. But he was more specific, and more insistent. He had stepped out on his porch for a moment that evening, and had seen a young lady with dark hair walking on the other side of the street. She had on a light dress and a hat and a shimmery shawl of some kind. He was too far away to see her face, but yes, he thought it had been Miss Bradford. She was the right height and she'd been wearing what they said she had on that night. Sheriff Royal repeatedly cross-questioned him as though with a perverse desire to find some flaw in his story, but the old man stubbornly held on to every detail, chilly evening or no. She was wearing a light-colored dress—yes, it might have been green, but he wouldn't say for sure; his eyes weren't *that* good—and a silver shawl. Well, not a *silver* shawl, he admitted when Royal pounced on him, but a silvery one, or shimmery one—something light like that. That's what he'd seen and that's all he could say. No other girl had admitted she was walking up Main

Street at that hour, had she? So who else could it be? Royal gave him up in disgust.

The baffling thing about both accounts was that Charity had been seen walking *up* Main Street—that is, away from Diana Lewis' shop and in the direction of Mrs. Henney's boarding-house—late that evening, a good three hours after she had first left Mrs. Henney's. If she had not been to Diana's shop, where had she been during all that time, and what had happened to her between the spot where the witnesses had seen her and the boarding-house where she had never arrived?

Randall Morris asked these questions over and over, in a way that seemed calculated to torture himself and to drive Andrew Royal to the limit of his already short patience. He hung over the sheriff's desk while Royal painstakingly made out a telegram in between telephoning to the other towns in the county that *had* a telephone, giving out a description of the girl and explaining when she had gone missing. Every word he spoke seemed gratingly halting and deliberate to Randall, and his stub of a pencil dithering and slow on the paper. When at last the telegram was completed Randall snatched the paper and raced his horse down to the depot to hand it over to the telegraph operator there, then back to the sheriff's office to announce that he was going to form a search party to go over the outlying farms and countryside, and to stipulate that a messenger should be sent to find him if there was any news of Charity.

When Randall had gone Andrew Royal ran his bony hands up through his thick gray hair until it all stood wildly on end, and then flattened it down again lest someone should come in and see it like that and guess that he was disturbed.

* * *

There was no need to send a messenger after Randall Morris that afternoon, and no news awaiting him when he returned to the office at dusk. The search party's efforts, which had produced nothing, were halted by the onset of darkness.

Morning brought pale sunshine, but shed no light on the fate of the missing girl. Randall Morris had not slept. His face was haggard and marked by strain.

"She must have been kidnapped," he said, giving voice for the first time to the thought that had been haunting him all along.

His eyes were fixed on the sheriff's face, but Royal did not look at him. But Randall's mute demand for acknowledgement in the silence that followed was more insistent than his speech, and the sheriff was forced to look up with exasperation.

Andrew Royal was a man who lived in undying terror of being thought soft-hearted or sentimental. In self-defense he cultivated a fierce moustache and a growling, annoyed manner that was always at its height when he felt most strongly. As he was most uncomfortable when around highly emotional people, Randall Morris was the last companion he would have chosen under these circumstances.

"Someone had to have taken her," Randall insisted. "She had no reason to go off by herself, in the middle of the night, without a change of clothes or even any money with her! Something's happened to her, Sheriff."

"You think I don't know that?" said Andrew Royal shortly.

"Can you just sit there and not do anything about it?" exploded Randall.

"Why don't you quit talking and start thinking?" Royal shot back. "If someone took her away from here, say in a wagon or buggy, by a road, they had all night to travel in the dark without being seen. If some harm had come to her nearer here...well, we'd have found some trace by now. But if anybody's seen her, or seen them, it'd have to be yesterday in the daylight, and by that time they'd have been far enough away from Sour Springs that word about a missing girl hasn't got there yet. You've got to give time for whoever might have spotted them to hear about it, and get word back. Eat something," he ordered, pointing with a jam-smeared knife to the remains of his breakfast, which he was eating at his desk according to custom.

"I can't." Randall shook his head miserably.

The sheriff had his mouth full once again, no doubt requiring some fortification after the longest speech he had made in the course of a year, when a man with a valise in his hand came up the street, looked at the sign over the open door and stepped into the office.

"Sheriff Royal?" he inquired, looking questioningly at the sheriff as he removed his hat. At Royal's brusque nod he came forward and took a card from his waistcoat pocket. "My name is Edgerton."

Andrew Royal glanced up from the card to the newcomer's face. "A detective?"

Edgerton nodded. He was a slim man of medium height, with close-cropped gray hair and serious, attentive gray eyes, dressed plainly but in clothes that spoke subtly of the city. "I'm hoping that you can provide me with some information."

"Oh," said Royal, glancing over at Randall Morris. Randall, who had been pacing the office when Edgerton arrived, had come quickly forward with dreading expectancy at his entrance, but turned away as abruptly when he heard the man's words. "Thought you were coming to give me some information. Maybe you hadn't heard, but there's a girl missing from here and I'm doing my *best* to find her." He accompanied the emphasis with another sharp glance in Randall's direction.

"Missing?" said Edgerton, looking from one to the other with unexpected attention. "What sort of girl?"

Andrew Royal rapped out the description he had given many times over the previous morning. "Five-feet-two, middling-dark brown hair, brown eyes, wearing a green dress and a hat with flowers and a shawl."

"Her name is Charity Bradford," Randall Morris supplied earnestly.

Edgerton set his valise down on the desk and stood with his hands resting on it. "A local girl? Has she any family here?"

Royal jerked a thumb toward Randall. "Just him. Randall Morris, Miss Bradford's intended."

Randall shook hands with Edgerton hurriedly. "She's been missing since the night before last, and I'm terribly worried about her. I know she didn't go off on her own. It's not like her."

"Then it was entirely unexpected? You hadn't noticed anything in her behavior recently — anything that suggested she might have something on her mind?"

"No. Why?" said Randall, suddenly becoming aware of the gravity in the detective's face.

"It's only, by some coincidence," said Edgerton, "that I'm looking for a young woman myself, one who fits your description of Miss Bradford quite closely. Certain information in my possession led me to believe that she might be found here, in Sour Springs."

"Charity?" said Randall. "I—I don't understand."

"The name of the girl I'm looking for, or at least the name we know her by, is Mary Taylor," said Edgerton, taking some papers from his valise and handing them over to Andrew Royal, who was listening frowningly. "Miss Taylor is wanted for questioning in New Orleans, where she was known to be the associate and accomplice of a man called John Faraday, an accomplished gentleman burglar and jewel thief. I've been on his trail for more than six years. He had a far-reaching and well-run organization, one of the curious features of which was that his various accomplices never had any contact with each other, only with Faraday himself.

"Miss Taylor's background is somewhat vague—she may have been on the stage or she may not, but that is immaterial—what we do know is that at different times and under different names she worked as companion to a wealthy elderly lady, as a fashionable milliner's assistant and a salesgirl in an expensive department store. In those capacities she helped to arrange and carry out a number of successful jewel thefts."

Edgerton clicked shut his valise. "A little over a year ago, Mr. Faraday had the misfortune to get himself shot in a street fracas in New Orleans. Shortly afterwards Miss Mary Taylor disappeared from view. There is a strong possibility that she had in her possession the fruits of their latest robbery, an extremely valuable pearl necklace. Since that time I've been trying to trace her. We've also been keeping an eye on several other people who are suspected of having worked with Faraday in the past. We know that one of them, who is now living in Denver, recently received a letter postmarked Sour Springs, Colorado."

"So that made you think this Taylor girl was here?" said Andrew Royal, jabbing a long forefinger on his desk to emphasize the location.

"It was a lead to follow up, at least, Sheriff. There is just the possibility that some of the others who worked with Faraday may now be in contact with Mary Taylor. At any rate, now I think you can understand my surprise at the seeming coincidence of a young woman who matches Miss Taylor's description suddenly disappearing, less than forty-eight hours before I arrived here in search of her."

"*Charity?*" repeated Randall Morris. "It's — it's impossible! You don't know her, Mr. Edgerton, or you'd realize what you're saying."

"How well do *you* know her?" asked Edgerton, turning to look the younger man in the eye. He spoke in a straightforward manner, but one not untouched with compassion, as one who knew what consequences the performance of his duty might have for others. "What can you tell me about her, Mr. Morris? What do you know about her background?"

"Just — that she has no family living," said Randall, still with incredulity, but the import of his own words beginning to creep in on him. "She had — she'd been on her own for a number of years — working for her living. I don't know how many."

"When did she come to Sour Springs?"

"A year ago."

"And you're engaged to be married? — How long have you been engaged?"

"Three months," said Randall. "We were going to be married in a few weeks."

"And you know nothing about her — where she was born, where she lived or how?"

"Look, Mr. Edgerton, you don't know what you're trying to do!" said Randall, putting his hands on the back of a chair and leaning over it as though he had suddenly found a need for support. "Charity's not that kind of girl. She just isn't. And if there was anything she'd — if she'd ever been in any kind of trouble, she would have told me."

Edgerton shook his head doubtfully. "She doesn't seem to have told you much of anything."

"Have you got a picture of that Taylor girl?" said Andrew Royal abruptly, having caught a glimpse of the look on Randall's face.

"Unfortunately, no," said Edgerton. "She apparently never had her photograph taken. All we have is a general description — a young woman between twenty and twenty-five years of age, brunette, attractive, with a ladylike, genteel appearance and manner."

"Charity to the letter," grumbled Royal under his breath.

Edgerton glanced at Randall Morris, and then addressed the sheriff. "Under the circumstances, if I could be allowed to examine Miss Bradford's home or lodgings, I might find something that would conclusively prove or disprove my suggestion, rather than pursuing this speculation; or possibly even find a clue to her whereabouts."

Royal raised his bushy eyebrows doubtfully, but as Randall spun around with an expression of outrage he brought them down grimly over his eyes again. Edgerton availed himself of the perceived advantage. "I am entirely willing to place myself under your direction, Sheriff, and to do only what you deem appropriate. I do think this course would be the most useful."

Sheriff Royal gave his usual exasperated exhalation, and started to climb up out of his chair. "Well, you won't lose anything by it," he said. "I don't guess I've got any objections, if Randall hasn't."

Edgerton turned with silent inquiry toward Randall. The younger man stood irresolute for a few seconds, the pain he felt reflected in his face, but he nodded shortly.

Andrew Royal gave a brief grunt of acknowledgement. "I'd better go right along with you," he said, "and deal with the landlady. I reckon it'll be better for everybody's feelings."

* * *

Mrs. Henney, in a considerable state of feeling herself, once more unlocked Charity's door for them. She remained in the doorway, her hands clasped nervously and her plump face drawn together in a piteous expression, as the two men surveyed the room. Andrew Royal, having turned about once with a belligerent look on his face, planted himself in the center of the room where he could keep an admonishing eye on the landlady and watch the detective's progress at the same time.

Edgerton knew his work. He raised the window-shade with a light touch, and looked around at the room by the better light. The single window was opposite the door; the head of the bed against the wall to the right of the window. The wardrobe stood against the right-hand wall, the mirrored bureau against the left. There was a single straight-backed chair, a braided rag rug on the floor and a few framed lithographs on the walls.

Edgerton conducted his search deftly, rapidly but without hurry. He examined the contents of the wardrobe, investigating pockets and feeling along the seams of garments where anything seemed likely to be concealed. He knelt to look beneath the bed and turned back the rug (Mrs. Henney assuring him that nothing could be hidden there, because she took it up to sweep every Thursday and Miss Charity and everyone in the house knew it). Then he turned his attention to the bureau. The agile fingers went through the contents of the drawers, the detective's gray eyes focused and his face expressionless.

He came at the last to a packet of letters in the topmost drawer, almost as if he had known all along that they would be there, and purposely left them to the last so the find would not distract his attention from any smaller matters in the room. He separated them with a hand as practiced as if he, and not Charity Bradford, had been accustomed to handle letters in a post-office.

He glanced briefly at and then laid aside a few short notes in a bold, slanting hand, signed "Randall." There were only a few more: a page of fine, stilted writing on questions of silk and beading from Diana Lewis;

another letter in a girl's hand from within Sour Springs. Lastly Edgerton singled out three letters folded together, written on a different type of paper than the others. He unfolded and read the first one, and a shadow came over his forehead.

He glanced significantly at Andrew Royal, and held out the letter. The sheriff drew nearer to him and read the first few words. He looked into the detective's eyes, and for once there was no mask over his bleak, weathered face.

Edgerton gave him the three letters, and while Royal was reading them over the detective folded the love-letters and the rest of the small, innocuous correspondence with considerate care, and laid them all back in the drawer.

* * *

The first letter ran:

Dear Miss Taylor,

I am writing to you in respect to the late Mr. Faraday, which it would do both of us good to meet and discuss. There are others besides myself who have an interest in that gentleman's affairs, but I think it would be more agreeable for you and I to come to an understanding regarding our respective interests before introducing these others into the discussion. I wait for your answer, respectfully,

A. N.

Edgerton re-read this carefully, standing in the dining-room of Mrs. Henney's boarding-house, while Randall Morris was reading with incomprehensible emotion the second of the trio, which the sheriff had just handed to him:

> *Dear Miss Taylor,*
> *I must insist that you give me a reply about the concerns of Mr. Faraday about which I communicated with you before. We do not accept your wish to avoid the subject, and want you to agree to a meeting where we can settle the matters once and for all. If you do not reply we will seek a personal answer. I will see you soon.*
> *A.N.*

Both of these letters were written with an apparent attempt at refinement, and a strenuous effort to convey a definite idea in vague terms, but in a round, uneducated-looking hand. The third, by contrast, had been printed, not written, and in haste:

> *Mary,*
> *There is an agent arrived from South. He may have a tip on the Johnson things. You are not the only one who can lose, so take no chances.*
> *A.N.*

"The 'Johnson things' are the pearls," said Edgerton. The three letters lay spread on the dining-room table. "The lady from whom they were stolen was named Johnson. How these people knew I was coming I don't know, but they must have been watching us while we've been watching them. It happened much as I figured. These 'others' evidently wanted a share in the money from the pearls, which Mary Taylor wasn't disposed to share, even though they sound like they were beginning to get quite insistent about it. But

it wouldn't be in their interest for her to be apprehended, either, so they warned her in time for her to
slip away before my arrival."

Randall Morris had not spoken a word since
Royal first showed him the letters. The look of bewilderment, disbelief and shock on his face was not
without its effect on the detective, who observed it
with silent sympathy.

Now Randall turned to him with a remnant of
energy, a defensive look battling to regain control on
his face. "These don't prove anything!" he said. "They
don't prove a thing. Someone could have put them in
her room."

"Who?" said Andrew Royal in a voice hard
with sarcasm.

"None of these are in Charity's handwriting,"
said Randall, his eyes fastened steadily on the
detective's quiet face, as Edgerton looked down at the
letters.

Edgerton inclined his head and admitted it.
"No, they're not. But —"

"Then they don't prove her connection with
those people. All you've got is that they were in her
room. Why couldn't someone have planted them
there?" He looked around at Royal. "Sour Springs is a
little town — everybody knows about everything here.
They notice the postmarks on everybody's letters. How
could Charity have gotten these without anyone
knowing about it?"

"She worked at the post-office," said Mrs.
Meade, who had come into the dining-room conference
so inconspicuously that none of the men had realized
that she had been sitting there for nearly the whole
time.

Edgerton regarded this apparition, of a kind-looking middle-aged lady in a brown dress, sitting with her hands folded decorously across her lap, with his signature expression of close attention modified by astonishment.

"I did not know that," he said after a moment. "I am much obliged, Mrs. —Miss —"

"Meade," grunted Andrew Royal.

"Mrs.," supplied Mrs. Meade, giving Edgerton her kindest smile. Her eyes twinkled with warm humor, and the detective smiled in spite of himself.

"Are you a friend of Mar —of Miss Bradford's, Mrs. Meade?"

"Oh, yes," said Mrs. Meade. "My room is just across the hall from hers, so naturally we see a good deal of each other. She's a very sweet girl —I've always been very fond of her."

"And yet —your remark about the post-office — forgive me, but it seems to support my theory that Miss Bradford is, in fact, Mary Taylor."

"I didn't say *that*," said Mrs. Meade with dismissive practicality. "I only noticed it. It *is* significant, I think."

"Good Lord, you don't mean to suggest she got herself hired on there on purpose?" said Andrew Royal even more crossly than was his wont.

"I think it means that...someone...thought of a great many details," said Mrs. Meade musingly, looking past Edgerton at the opposite wall.

There was a few seconds' silence, and then Edgerton said, reaching for one of the letters on the table, "Was there anything else that you noticed about these letters, Mrs. Meade?"

"I thought it was amusing the way the writer of

the second letter varied between referring to himself as 'I' and 'we'," said Mrs. Meade, smiling again. "It made me imagine several people gathered around a table, all trying to tell the writer what to say and probably arguing among themselves as they did it."

Edgerton laughed. "I did observe the varying pronouns, but I hadn't put quite such a vivid construction on them. I do agree with you, though, Mrs. Meade—I believe there are a number of people concerned in this." He made a slight gesture with the letter in his hand.

"Perhaps that is what makes it so difficult," said Mrs. Meade thoughtfully.

Edgerton looked attentively at her for a moment, a curious look on his face, and then he seemed to recall himself to his present task. He glanced down at the letter in his hand, gathered the other two up from the table and folded them together, and then he passed around the table and stopped by Andrew Royal's chair. "For the present," he said in a quiet voice, "it seems your investigation and mine have the same object, Sheriff. I think it would be advantageous to us both to work together, at least until Miss Bradford is found."

Royal did not seem to hear for a moment. Then he gave a sort of start, and with a grumble of acquiescence, he got up from the table and pushed his chair back into its place with a big booted foot in a manner that would have made Mrs. Henney's eyes pitifully round if she had been there to see.

* * *

Randall Morris sat alone at the table in the empty kitchen, his head in his hands. He ran unsteady fingers through his hair and drew a quivering breath. He was stunned by the reality of all he had heard, but in his heart still clung to the belief that somehow it was all wrong. Whatever the proofs, he could not believe it.

Charity...his beautiful, dainty Charity, with her deep brown eyes that shone up at him as though she had never loved anyone so well before. Had all her goodness, her quiet charm and modesty, been the playing of a part? He would never believe that she had not truly loved him. But were the other things true? A thief—a criminal? He pushed the thought of the man named John Faraday far away from his mind; he could not bear that.

Mrs. Meade came into the kitchen. She cast a look at the kettle on the back of the stove, thinking perhaps about whether a cup of tea might be of any value in this situation, but decided against it and sat down at the table. She looked at Randall Morris, but he did not see or hear her, though he may have been vaguely aware of her presence.

It was true—he knew practically nothing of Charity's past. That had never mattered to him before; he had never given it a thought. Now he could not escape the idea. Had Charity really been reserved—avoided the subject of her own life—or was it only that he had never asked any questions?

He saw her now, her delicate figure and profile outlined in soft moonlight as she had sat beside him on a summer night in Mrs. Henney's trim little garden outside the boarding-house. A yellow glow came through the old lace curtains on the open windows, accompanied by the flutter of the ladies' voices in the parlor, while all around them the moonlight, the clear breath of the night air touched with the scent of the flowers, the tiny pipings of crickets and the whisper of breezes and other night insects, combined to make a night of such palpable loveliness that for a while neither of them spoke, wanting only to be silent and savor its rare beauty and the consciousness of each other's presence.

At length, he had heard Charity give a soft, pensive sigh.

"What's the matter?" he said, looking down at her. "That sounded almost unhappy."

"Oh, no…I'm not unhappy," said Charity, resting her head against his arm, and looking up at the slate-blue moonlit sky. "How could I be? But some-times—sometimes to be happy like this is almost painful."

Randall laughed, putting his arm around her and drawing her closer to him. "Happiness doesn't hurt. I've tried it, and I know."

"It isn't the happiness," said Charity, a little smile playing about her lips; the influence of his personality that she could never resist. "It's re-membering what it used to be like before, when I had no one to—to really care anything about me. Life was like that for so long that it makes now—tonight—seem too wonderful to be true." Her wide eyes searched the vista of trees and sky. When she spoke again her voice was nearly a whisper. "Whenever I see a night like this, I feel that I'll never see one like it again."

"Then don't remember, if it hurts you," said Randall gently.

Charity sighed again. "I don't always re-member because I want to."

"It'll fade after you've been happy long enough, darling. One day those memories will be so far off they won't have the power to hurt you." He looked down into her eyes. "You believe that, don't you?"

"I do," she said.

And then he had put his fingertips under her chin and lifted her face and kissed her, and Charity had clung to him as though trying to erase as many memories as possible with one moment's bliss.

Randall put his face down in his folded arms on the kitchen table. He had never been more wrong than he had been on that summer night. It was memories of happiness that hurt worst, when the thing itself was torn away from you.

Mrs. Meade sat very still. Her gaze rested gently on Randall's tousled brown head, but wisely, she did not speak. She lifted her head to look away at the kitchen wall, and for a moment her bright eyes were dim, and old.

Mrs. Meade, childless all her life, was not a woman who made much of her widowhood, or expounded much on her past joys or sorrows. Those who did not know her well, or had not the capacity to know anyone well, might have thought the cheerfulness with which she went through life was a lack of deeper feeling. But she still held in her heart, ten years after her last parting with him, a deep and precious affection for the husband who stared out of the faded photograph that stood on her bureau. There were remembrances both bitter and sweet tucked away in the pages of her own little history, a record not on display for all the world to read. Hers was a heart that knew many things, and a heart that did not forget.

Randall slowly lifted his head, and Mrs. Meade

saw that his eyelashes were wet as he blinked unsteadily.

He looked toward her, and she smiled. "You mustn't let your mind run away with you," she said.

Randall shook his head. "She would have told me," he said. "She loved me—she *trusted* me. I know that. I could *feel* it." His eyes fixed entreatingly on Mrs. Meade's gentle, sensible face. "*You* don't believe it, do you, Mrs. Meade?"

"No, I do not," said Mrs. Meade with emphasis. "Even though I have no real reason to be so sure. I don't believe it."

"Then do you think someone deliberately put those letters in Charity's room?"

"How could someone have gotten into Charity's room?" said Mrs. Meade. "Even supposing— merely supposing, of course!—that it was someone who lived in this house, who might have had a chance to step in unnoticed—the door was locked. The only person with a spare key was Mrs. Henney, whom I think we can safely discount! The letters could only have been introduced into the room after Charity's disappearance, or she would sooner or later have discovered them in her bureau drawer. But she locked her bedroom door upon going out that evening, and it was still locked when we tried it the next morning."

"But it had to have been whoever kidnapped her. That's what I thought from the first. Charity had the keys to the house and her room in her bag—they used those to get in."

Mrs. Meade shook her head. "I don't think so, Randall. If it was the kidnapper, they would have had to know all about this Mary Taylor business well beforehand, which would have been rather extraordinary."

"But *someone* put those letters there," said Randall doggedly.

"Yes," said Mrs. Meade. "I think we should assume that. It would be a little strange, don't you think—if Charity really was Mary Taylor—that she should run away to escape being apprehended, and yet leave such plain evidence of her identity behind?"

"Good gosh, that's right!" cried Randall. "I never thought of that. Didn't Edgerton see that?"

"I don't blame him for not seeing it," said Mrs. Meade. "He found what he was expecting to find, exactly where he expected to find it, so of course it all made sense to him. But still…"

She tapped two fingers thoughtfully on the edge of the table. "Do you know, I would like to take a look around that room myself. I don't know why, but I have a feeling there must be something…"

"Something Edgerton missed, you mean?"

"No, I don't think he missed anything. He is, I think, a very intelligent man. But perhaps there was something he didn't know he was looking for."

She rose from the table, and Randall stood up too, looking at her with doubtful hope. Mrs. Meade patted his arm with a reassuring gesture as she stepped past him toward the kitchen doorway. "I think I shall ask Mrs. Henney if we may use the key again—just to see…"

* * *

Mrs. Meade looked slowly about Charity's room. It was the same as she had seen it many times. Something of the personality of the girl who had lived there seemed to hang over it still, lending an intangible soft charm to the plain, sparse furniture and the few simple decorations. But it was quiet—pitifully quiet without its occupant.

She turned in a circle, her eyes marking and considering each object in the room as they reached it. Randall Morris watched her from a few steps back, and Mrs. Henney stood clasping her ring of keys in the doorway.

Mrs. Meade's gaze directed itself thoughtfully toward the wardrobe, as it had done on the previous morning. She moved around the foot of the bed and opened the doors. For a moment she looked at the clothes hanging inside, and then she turned to look at Randall.

"Suppose for a moment that Mr. Edgerton's theory was correct—that Charity left of her own accord, to avoid meeting him," she said. "If that was so, when she went somewhere other than Miss Lewis' shop that night, she must have met someone, received a warning or discussed plans—but then she *came back here*. Two people saw her walking in this direction. If she were planning to leave town she could only have been coming back here to gather some of her possessions. But none of her clothes are missing. That isn't right. Why didn't she take them?"

"Because she didn't come back here. She was kidnapped," said Randall.

"Yes…but there is still the question of where she was, those three hours…" Mrs. Meade was looking down at the hatbox on the floor of the wardrobe. "Did Mr. Edgerton put everything back just as he found it, Mrs. Henney?"

"Why, yes—everything exactly. He was very

careful," said Mrs. Henney mournfully.

Mrs. Meade bent and picked up the hatbox, moving as if to look underneath it, but something halted her — drew her attention to the box itself in her hands. She gave it a slight shake. Turning around, she set it on the bed and lifted the lid. She took out a small thick bundle of knitted material, and carefully unfolded it. It fell open in her hands, a light triangular shawl in a soft shade of green.

Mrs. Meade looked over at the landlady. "Mrs. Henney — did you put this in here?"

"Why, no, I didn't," said Mrs. Henney with a gasp. "I haven't touched a thing in this room, not since Miss Charity left."

"Was it here when Mr. Edgerton searched the room?"

Mrs. Henney's eyes looked as if they could not possibly grow any bigger. "Why, yes — yes, it was. I saw him open the hatbox, and look all inside it. He folded it up neatly when he was done."

Mrs. Meade looked across the bed at Randall Morris, the shawl still held up before her. "But this shawl was not in the hatbox when I looked in the wardrobe yesterday morning. The box was empty when I lifted it then — I could feel the difference at once when I lifted it again just now." She held the shawl out to the light. "This is the shawl Charity was wearing when she went out the other night, isn't it, Mrs. Henney?"

Mrs. Henney could hardly breathe. "The very same, Mrs. Meade! She always wore it with her green gingham — the very same color."

"Then someone put this shawl into the hatbox between the time I touched it yesterday morning, and the time you saw Mr. Edgerton examine it today."

"Someone—in this room? In my house?" shrilled Mrs. Henney.

"The kidnapper!" said Randall, to whom the quaking landlady might as well not have existed.

"Of course not," was Mrs. Meade's somewhat surprising answer. "Why would they go to all that trouble when they could simply keep it with them? Supposing they *were* the one who put those letters in the drawer—if the shawl was found here too, it would betray that someone else had been in the room. If they wished Charity to be identified as Mary Taylor they wouldn't want that."

"Then—it *wasn't* whoever brought the letters?" said Randall, who was beginning to flounder out of his depth.

Mrs. Meade did not answer at once. She moved slowly around the bed, still turning over the light shawl in her hands, and stopped by the window. She stood for a moment gazing through it, but not seeing anything outside.

"No," she said at last, "it was done by someone who did not want this shawl found in their possession—and that person also put the letters in the drawer." There was an unusual firmness about her voice as she spoke, and her fingers tightened on the folds of the shawl in an odd way. "Their reason for getting rid of the shawl...was strong enough for them to risk its being connected with the letters."

"In—in this room? Someone came into my house?" quavered Mrs. Henney again.

"At night," said Mrs. Meade. "No one in this house ever heard Charity come in late at night, did they? They came in the same way."

"In my house? At night? How did they get into my house?" Mrs. Henney was nearly beside herself.

"With Charity's keys," said Mrs. Meade.

"But—I thought you said it wasn't the kidnapper," said Randall, staring.

"It wasn't," said Mrs. Meade.

The stunned silence that followed this remark was broken in a wholly unexpected manner.

"I believe I have some errands to run," said Mrs. Meade briskly. She laid the shawl across the foot of the bed and walked straight to the door. "Thank you for the use of the key, Mrs. Henney."

She vanished into the hall, and Randall Morris and the landlady were left staring after her in bewilderment.

Randall came slowly out into the hall, and Mrs. Henney followed and locked the bedroom door behind them, stealing an awed and sympathetic look after the young man. They were both too amazed by Mrs. Meade's sudden change in manner, and the apparently unconcerned way in which she had put the question of Charity's fate behind her, to think of their own troubles, grave as they had seemed a moment before.

Mrs. Meade emerged from her own room, adjusting her hat. "Good afternoon, Mrs. Henney—I will be back in a little while," she said as she started down the front stairs. Randall trailed after her mechanically, the fog of confused depression settled about him again.

At the foot of the stairs Mrs. Meade paused and turned to wait for him. When he joined her she laid her hand on his arm and beckoned him to bend his head down, and when he did so she murmured something in his ear. He gave her a quick, startled look.

Mrs. Meade nodded. "Yes," she said. "But don't make much noise about it, do you understand? Good. Now I must be going."

* * *

Mrs. Meade mounted the stairs to the second floor above Benton's dry-goods store and rapped at the closed door. After a moment, the sound of a woman's footsteps approached from within and Diana Lewis opened the door.

"Good afternoon, Miss Lewis," said Mrs. Meade. "I have a question for you — some work I would like you to help me with. May I come in?"

Diana Lewis gave a deferential nod and stood aside for her to enter, and Mrs. Meade stepped into the room. It was a pleasant place, with long windows admitting the sunlight through the branches of a tall tree just outside. A sewing-machine stood in the corner, and by the windows were a sofa and several chairs for the accommodation of clients. At the far end of the room a door stood ajar, offering a glimpse of the work-room in back and the couch that could be made up into a bed at night.

Mrs. Meade had paused and stood looking at a white silk dress that was displayed on a mannequin near the end of the front room. The beautiful, intricate beaded embroidery on the yoke was nearly finished; there remained only some finishing touches on the sleeves and the flounces on the skirt to complete.

Diana Lewis shut the door and waited with her hands folded in front of her. She was a slim, dark girl, with a rather pretty face, but with the tired eyes and faded complexion that spoke of ill health and much time spent indoors. But in spite of any infirmity she was an exquisite seamstress. Charity Bradford's was the first wedding-dress she had made in Sour Springs, and half the female population had already manufactured errands to her shop in hopes of catching a glimpse of its progress.

Mrs. Meade turned away from contemplating it. "I would like your advice on a pattern, Miss Lewis," she said. "You see, the daughter of a dear friend of mine is going to be married soon, and I want to send her a gift. She will have so many nice things, so I would like it to be — not something large, but special. I was thinking of — a shawl. Something like that lovely embroidered brocade shawl of yours would be just perfect. May I look at it?"

"Yes, of course," said Diana Lewis, after what might have been just a second's pause. "I can make up a pattern for you to follow, Mrs. Meade. It's very simple, really — "

"Oh, but I would like to look at your shawl before I begin — the embroidery on the edges is so lovely, I would like to see what stitches you used. It won't take a moment." She smiled in such a happy expectant way that Diana Lewis could not help smiling slightly herself, though she did not seem wholly pleased. "I'm sorry, Mrs. Meade, but — I don't believe I have it here this morning."

Mrs. Meade's eyes grew innocently wide, in what a sharp observer might have recognized with amusement as an excellent imitation of Mrs. Henney. "Why, I don't believe I have ever seen you without it in the summertime. You wear it here to your work every day, don't you?"

"Really, this once I must have forgotten it. I've

left it at home. But that is no difficulty; I can make up the pattern for you when I go home and send it to you in a few days."

"But there's no time like the present!" said Mrs. Meade brightly. A happy thought seemed to strike her, and she fairly clasped her hands with pleasure. "Why not let me go to your boarding-house and fetch it for you now? I have errands to run, and —"

"No — Mrs. Meade, please don't trouble yourself," said Diana Lewis. She twisted her thin hands tighter together.

"Oh, it's no trouble! I —"

"Mrs. Meade, please — I would much rather you did not."

She stopped, conscious of her words having fallen rather loud and abruptly in the stillness that followed them.

Mrs. Meade gave her a penetrating look. All her affected lightness of manner had gone. "Because it is not at your boarding-house, after all — is it, Miss Lewis?'

"I beg your pardon?" said Diana.

Mrs. Meade's voice was still quiet, but inflexible. "Because you do not have the shawl. You gave it to Charity…didn't you?"

There was another second's pause, distinct this time. "I — don't understand you," said Diana Lewis.

"Oh, you do," Mrs. Meade assured her.

Before Diana Lewis could summon any words to answer, there came a confused noise of feet on the stairs, and then a loud knock at the door.

"Come in," said Mrs. Meade in a clear voice.

It was Sheriff Royal who entered, with a harassed expression that declared belligerently to all the world that he was there on compulsion. "What's going on?" he demanded with no attempt at ceremony.

"Well! I'm glad you decided to come, Andrew. I rather thought you'd object. And Mr. Edgerton," added Mrs. Meade, looking past him to where the detective stood in the doorway, with Randall Morris behind him.

Since the sheriff seemed to have been struck mute by Mrs. Meade's salutation, she added simply, with a gesture toward the young lady in question, "I should like for you to meet Miss Mary Taylor."

Diana Lewis' face had turned a duller shade of white, but she did not move or speak. She looked at Edgerton as he stepped into the room, surveying her with the amazement that all Mrs. Meade's actions seemed to call up in him.

"Miss Lewis, the seamstress?—Are you...are you very sure, Mrs. Meade?" he managed to say, being, for once in his successful career, unable to think of anything more to the point.

"Oh, yes. Very sure. It was the shawl, you see," Mrs. Meade explained.

"Yes—Randall told me about it. That is, he said something about your finding a shawl, but I'm afraid I don't quite understand the significance of it."

"Well," said Mrs. Meade, "to begin with, we have all been relying a good deal on Miss Lewis' statement, haven't we? That Charity never came to her shop that night. Really Miss Lewis told a simple untruth: Charity *did* come here that night as usual. You see, if her shawl were to be found in Miss Lewis' possession that would immediately give the lie to her story. So she had to get rid of it. Charity's little purse and its contents were small enough to be destroyed or scattered, perhaps, but she could not dispose of the shawl that quickly. She was uneasy, perhaps; worrying that at length it might occur to someone to question the truth of her story and examine her shop or lodgings. So she took something of a risk, and returned the shawl to Charity's room at Mrs. Henney's."

"How?" blurted Andrew Royal very loudly, and then immediately looked as though he would have liked to disappear on the spot.

"She had the keys to the house and room from Charity's purse. All she had to do was go quietly enough not to wake the household, and not show a light. That was what attracted my notice to the hatbox. It was several inches to the right of where it had been when I saw it yesterday morning, and half on top of a flat parcel in the bottom of the wardrobe. Mrs. Henney said that Mr. Edgerton put everything back the way he found it — and I quite believed you would be so precise, Mr. Edgerton — so that meant someone else had moved it. Mrs. Henney said she had not. I thought perhaps someone could have taken it out and put it back in the dark, not quite able to see where they were placing it."

"I suppose the fault lies with me," said Edgerton, smiling a little, "for not recognizing the oddity of a shawl kept in a hatbox in the first place."

"Of course not," returned Mrs. Meade. "Women keep all manner of things in odd places. I once knew a young lady who kept novels and sweetmeats in a hatbox, and got away with it, too — most likely because she shared them with her maid. But what you didn't see was the significance of the shawl itself — it was green."

"Green?"

"Yes. Mrs. Henney in her perturbation didn't

notice when she saw you handling it, but when I showed her later she immediately recognized it, as I myself did, as the shawl Charity was wearing the day she disappeared. But it wasn't the one she was wearing when she was seen on Main Street that night! Old Mr. Hawkins was right—he really did see a 'silver' or 'shimmery' shawl. That sounded odd to me when I first heard about it, but I didn't understand it then. But when I found the green one in the hatbox and realized why it was there, I remembered a certain white brocade shawl immediately recognizable as belonging to Miss Diana Lewis. A green knitted shawl isn't shimmery. What Mr. Hawkins saw was white silk brocade, shining in the light from some nearby window."

Randall Morris broke in: "But Mrs. Meade— *where is Charity?*"

"She *was* kidnapped," said Mrs. Meade, "but for a very odd reason—because she was *mistaken* for Mary Taylor—or rather, Diana Lewis."

"Ha!" said Edgerton explosively, the glint in his eye betokening instant comprehension and admiration.

"Yes. Miss Lewis deliberately arranged to have Charity taken for her. That was the reason for the exchange of shawls, which she somehow contrived while Charity was here with her. If you will inquire among the ladies of this town you will find that no one else has a shawl quite like that white one. And there *is* a resemblance of sorts between Charity Bradford and Diana Lewis. They are both nearly the same height, slight and dark-haired—in short, the description you had to follow. In the dark, with that shawl to guide them, who might not be mistaken?"

"I don't know how you know these things, Mrs.

Meade, but every moment I find myself more disposed to believe you," said Edgerton. "Miss Lewis—you have heard what has been said. Do you have any kind of explanation to offer?"

The seamstress turned away from him. Her former taut, nerve-bound expression was already gone, now that she saw there was nothing for her to do; her attitude expressed only a sort of resigned indifference.

"Yes," she said in a voice that held no regret, or even distress at her failure; "yes, it's true—I am Mary Taylor...or at least that is the name you call me."

"And Charity Bradford? What has happened to her, and why?"

"May I sit down? I am not strong, you know." She swallowed and moistened her lips, as though her mouth was dry.

Edgerton inclined his head curtly, and Diana Lewis sat down on the sofa by the window. Mrs. Meade, in the meantime, took uninvited possession of one of the easy-chairs and placed her reticule and her two hands in her lap, ready to listen attentively.

Diana Lewis began in the same flat voice, "I left New Orleans because I had received letters from people I did not want to meet...other associates of Mr. Faraday's. You know about him, I imagine...yes. They wanted certain things of his that they believed I had in my possession." She swallowed again. "I—I did not want to see them. I couldn't get rid of the jewels on my own—and I didn't have the courage to simply throw them away. It was the weakness of my old life. But I wanted to get away, and begin something entirely different. But the letters kept coming, and they gradually became threatening. So I left the city. These people didn't know me by sight, and I wanted to keep it so. I traveled under assumed names, and wore a veil or a hat that shaded my face, so that if they did manage to trace me they would not have a distinct impression of what I looked like. They would hardly be so foolish as to molest an unknown woman if they were not sure of her identity."

"But did you know the people who were following you? Could you recognize them?"

"We had never met, but I had heard at least one of them described. After leaving the city I never was sure if I saw any of them — but I sometimes had the feeling of being followed."

"Why didn't you simply turn the jewels over to them, if you didn't care about having them yourself?" said Edgerton, frowning.

"Because I was afraid, I tell you — I believed they would kill me after I had given them the jewels, to prevent my incriminating them in the future. I had answered their letters — I had unwisely made some remarks about wanting to be done with my past life that made them think I could not be trusted. I knew what they were capable of and I had every reason to fear the worst."

She stopped, out of breath, clenching her thin fingers together in her lap. She lifted her head and began again, unevenly: "When I reached Sour Springs I believed I had escaped them. I lived here quietly for a few months, and then one day I saw a man on the street — a man who matched the description I had heard, who seemed to be watching me. I managed to stay far enough away from him to keep him from seeing my face. The next night I saw from my window the shadow of a man lurking by the gate. I began to be desperately afraid."

"And so," said Edgerton, with a hard sarcasm that none of the others had thought to see from him, "you arranged to put an innocent girl into their power in your place."

"I only meant it to buy a little time! By the time they were convinced of their mistake I meant to be gone from Sour Springs, and not let them trace me again. I didn't mean Charity any harm. I chose her because of the superficial resemblance between us, as Mrs. Meade has said, and because she had reason to frequently come to my shop in the evening. I began wearing light-colored dresses similar to hers; I re-trimmed my hat in the same fashion as the one she wore; I did my hair the same way she did hers. I imitated her way of walking. I was an actress once, you know.

"All this time I was careful to walk outside only in broad daylight, when there were people around me, and to go nowhere but my shop and back to my boarding-house. I kept my face shaded...and I wore a distinctive shawl. The shawl...the most important part of all." A strange light came into her eyes. "I had de-termined that only the house where I was staying was watched; my shop was in too busy a street for them to risk anything there.

"The night before last Charity came here to work as usual. While she was busy I managed to ab-stract her shawl and hide it. When it had grown completely dark I said I had left some material for her wedding-dress at home, and asked Charity if she could go and bring it, since I was not feeling well enough for the walk. When she could not find her shawl at once, I offered to lend her mine."

Mrs. Meade's lips were pinched very tightly

together. She looked at Randall Morris, who all this time had stood opposite the sofa, staring in horrified incredulity at the seamstress as her flat, listless voice laid out the whole of the sickeningly practical design. As Diana Lewis pronounced these last words the image rose before his eyes of a girl turning into a quiet darkened lane, the white shawl around her shoulders shining in a ghostly fashion in the dusk. As she reached the garden gate of a silent house and put out her hand to open it, a black figure separated itself from the other shadows and moved behind her...until at the last instant some instinct made her sense another, silent presence, but even as she whipped around startled it was too late —

For an instant his mind reeled. His voice shook as he said, low and fiercely, "Where is she?"

"I don't know," said Diana Lewis. "She didn't come back. That is all I can tell you."

"I don't think so, Miss Lewis! You'd better tell us more and a good deal more, or I swear I'll —"

"Now that's enough," said Andrew Royal, putting out a hand to stop Randall as he made a threatening move forward. "Charity's all right. They think she's Mary Taylor, they won't harm her till she tells them where those pearls are — and she *can't.*"

"But they will find the pearls," observed Diana Lewis, "because Charity has them."

The three men simultaneously drew a sharp breath, and then — "What?" said Edgerton.

"The pearls are on the white shawl. I hid them among the pearl beads of the embroidery on the edges."

"I always *did* think that elaborate shawl was questionable taste for everyday wear," observed Mrs.

Meade, "which was especially odd, since you have always had such good taste otherwise."

The delayed reaction of the men burst all at once. Between Edgerton's "You did what?" and Royal's "Now you've torn it!" Randall's voice rose hoarsely. "Where did they take her? You tell me that now or I'll kill you myself!"

"Now, *really*, Randall," said Mrs. Meade mildly, but not at all as if she thought he meant it.

Edgerton interposed himself into the forefront of the scene, speaking in rapid, businesslike fashion. "Give me the names, descriptions, and any other information you have about these people you believe responsible, and if Miss Bradford is found unharmed I'll do what I can on your behalf in court — as difficult as I find it to feel any sympathy for you," he added, in a purely personal capacity.

"I don't know any names," said Diana Lewis. "The one man I've seen is medium height — thin — he has a narrow hooked nose, and most often wears a woolen scarf around his neck. As for the others — I believe there are two, or maybe three — I received the impression that there is another man and his wife."

"That's them," said Edgerton. "Thank God, we *were* on the right track. I believe I can put my hands on them."

"Who?" demanded Andrew Royal.

Edgerton, apparently not hearing him, spoke to Randall Morris. "It's only a question of time now, and I think we've got time on our side. I'll wire my colleague in Denver, who's been shadowing this suspicious married couple, and then take a fast train to meet him. I'll have his reply sent to one of the stops along the line. Are you coming?"

"You bet your life," said Randall. "Do you know where they are?"

"My colleague will know where they've been, at any rate. The only thing that worries me is that they know they're being watched — I'm remembering that third letter."

"You needn't worry about that," said Mrs. Meade. "They never wrote that letter. Miss Lewis wrote it herself."

"How do you know that?" exclaimed Edgerton, not even bothering to question the possibility of her statement this time.

"Why, what other reason is there to suddenly begin printing when you've been writing, other than to disguise handwriting? Only, of course, it was Miss Lewis who wanted to disguise hers — those other people weren't worried about who would see their letters. And they certainly didn't want Mary Taylor to flee if they were planning to kidnap her."

"Let's go," said Edgerton to Randall, casting a hasty look at his watch. "Sheriff, will you maintain custody of Miss Lewis until —"

"I most surely will not," said Andrew Royal. "I'm not going to be kept out of this. I've got a deputy that can keep Miss Lewis company here till we get back — boy needs something to keep him busy anyway."

* * *

A burning red sunset colored the sky over the city, seeming to bring it lower, like a heavy canopy stretched from mountaintop to mountaintop. Wisps of cloud, ever changing in shape, slowly dissolved and then regathered themselves high up in the still, glowing air.

Edgerton's colleague, another unobtrusive man in plain clothes, emerged from the shadows at a street corner and joined their party, which already included a member of the Denver police force.

"Early this afternoon," he said in response to Edgerton's mute glance of inquiry. "Two men and a woman."

"One woman?" said Edgerton. "It might be, but…could you see what she looked like?"

"No, she had on a long cloak and hood."

The street they turned into was narrower than the last, and the sharp shadows of houses that crossed it and met in the middle made it look as if it narrowed to a point and disappeared. But they reached this point, passed it and were cloaked in shadow themselves.

Randall Morris never remembered afterward where he had been or what he had seen. His mind was too full and too agitated to receive any further impressions of sight or sound. He was only conscious of the looming shapes of buildings that seemed to lean in on either side, black against the lurid glow of the red sky. The scene in the dark lane at Sour Springs was constantly repeating itself in his mind, blotting out all else like a spill of ink each time it came up.

They stopped before a certain house. A second policeman left the shadow at the side of it to join them. "The second floor, sir," he said in a low voice to Edgerton's colleague.

Edgerton noiselessly opened the door giving onto the street, and they passed in one after the other. He led the way up a dark, narrow set of stairs, and they followed cautiously, stepping as lightly as possible to avoid betraying their presence. Andrew Royal's harsh breathing made more sound than all their feet put together.

In the upstairs hall the two detectives drew near a closed door and listened; from behind it was coming the sound of several suppressed voices in rapid argument. Edgerton very carefully tried the knob; it was locked. He motioned to the two policemen, who moved to the forefront.

The door burst in with a crash and two men who had been sitting at a table leaped to their feet, while a woman who had been standing near looked across at the intruders with a fleeting mechanical expression of alarm, but had not even time to draw back a step. Randall saw all this in a second's confused glimpse; was aware of the rush forward by the invading party and heard Edgerton's sharp voice calling out to the inhabitants not to move, that they were under arrest. But he only half heard and half saw, for he was looking for just one thing. He made straight across the room and burst into the one behind it. A single candle standing on a night-table wavered wildly and went out in the gust from the door. The red sunset light was coming in through the dusty panes of a small window. A girl in a light gingham dress was half lying at the head of the narrow bed, her wrists bound with a handkerchief, her frightened brown eyes staring up at him from above the gag that covered her mouth.

In seconds she was freed and clasped to his heart. Her faint, sobbing cry of relief was muffled against him as he held her close, held her for a long moment.

Edgerton stopped in the doorway and looked

in for an instant; having thus briefly assured himself of Charity's safety he disappeared again into the outer room.

Randall, for once in his life, was succinct. "Come on," he said steadily, and with his supporting arms still around her he led her toward the door.

The three prisoners were in handcuffs, and Andrew Royal, finding himself superfluous to the operation, was making up for it by suspiciously supervising everyone else. He looked at Charity's white face as she leaned half fainting against Randall. "Get her out of here!" he growled.

He became aware that Edgerton was going round the room like a dog on a scent, and divining his purpose, began to look hurriedly about himself. "Where is it?" he barked at the hard-faced woman who stood straight and silent with her hands in irons. Without waiting for an answer he stomped toward the other room. Edgerton saw him and immediately made after him; but he was a few seconds too late, and it was Andrew Royal who drew from a dingy carpetbag that had been thrown aside on a chair in the bedroom the crumpled folds of a white silk shawl.

* * *

The next morning found brilliant sunshine sparkling in at the windows of the train racing back toward Sour Springs. Four were seated by a window, the warm sunbeams flicking over them, discussing the events of the past two days.

Charity had recovered somewhat from her ordeal, but the effects of what she had been through were still evident in her slightly pale face and soft, subdued voice, and she remained close to Randall's side. Edgerton and Royal sat opposite them. Charity was recounting to them the details of her experience.

"I hadn't any idea what it was all about," she said, "and that's what made it so frightening. I couldn't seem to make them understand that my name was not Mary Taylor, that I had never even heard of such a person. They seemed determined not to listen to me."

"The real Mary Taylor would undoubtedly have said the same," said Edgerton, "which is why they took no stock in your protestations."

"But who *was* Mary Taylor really, Mr. Edgerton? What did she do?"

Randall had only given Charity a brief, hurried explanation the night before of the circumstances surrounding her abduction, so she had yet to hear the story of Diana Lewis' treachery. Edgerton explained more fully now, beginning with his own labor in tracing the jewel thieves, up through the revelations of the previous day. Charity listened with a serious, interested expression that gradually gave way to astonishment.

"Then there really *were* pearls?" she said slowly when he concluded.

"Very valuable ones, Miss Bradford." Edgerton put out his hand and took up a fold of the white silk shawl, which reposed at that moment on Andrew Royal's knee. He would have liked to take the whole garment, but found the other end still held firmly in the sheriff's grasp. Royal had determinedly maintained possession of the shawl all night and all morning, despite many similar attempts on Edgerton's part to draw it away from him; evidently bound to hang on to his one share in the business for as long as possible.

"Do you see the larger ones here and there among these pearl beads? You might not be able to tell the difference, other than the size, but an expert would tell you that they're the real thing."

Charity leaned forward and put out her hand to touch the glistening hem of the shawl. "And I had them all the time, and never knew it!"

"Didn't any of the kidnappers see the beads? One would think, with pearls uppermost in their mind, it would have caught their notice at once."

"Or that *I* would have noticed, since they kept questioning me about pearls so insistently! No, no one did. It was dark at first—and when they made me put on that dark cloak to avoid anyone noticing us, one of the men shoved the shawl into that carpetbag, and it wasn't taken out again until you found it."

Charity's fingertips rested on the edge of the brocade for a moment, a slight shadow touching her face. "It all still seems so incredible," she said. "I—I can hardly believe that Diana would do such a thing to me."

"I found it hard to comprehend at first myself, Miss Bradford," said Edgerton. He leaned forward in his seat, resting his elbows on his knees, and looked over at Randall Morris. "Do you know, I have the oddest feeling of having bungled this entire investigation, in spite of the fact that we've succeeded in every way. I suppose that, following our original line of reasoning, we would have traced the supposed 'Mary Taylor' to Faraday's old associates in time. But we'd never have happened on Diana Lewis! And the way Mrs. Meade so quickly uncovered the kidnapping plot undoubtedly saved Miss Bradford much more danger and harm, by getting us there so soon—quite possibly, Miss Bradford, even saved your life."

Charity's hand tightened in the one of Randall's that held it as he said, "Mrs. Meade—God bless her! She had her head on straight the whole time, when the rest of us were going round in circles."

Edgerton nodded. "I really can't think of any commendation high enough. You know, I've thought myself a fairly proficient detective, but they do say that woman's intuition—"

"Woman's intuition nothing," said Andrew Royal shortly. "That twittering hen of a Henney woman didn't see a thing when you flapped the evidence around right under her nose. Women aren't created equal."

Edgerton was hard put to it, for a moment, to keep from laughing.

He looked across at the other two. It was perhaps something he saw in their faces that prompted his next speech.

He stood up and looked out of the window. "It looks like a beautiful morning," he said. "Since that's the case, Sheriff—suppose you join me on the platform for a breath of air?"

"Air!" said Andrew Royal, staring at him in frank amazement.

"Yes," said Edgerton, taking him by the arm. "You'll find it invigorating, I'm sure. You've been through a great deal, you know, Sheriff, and you could do with a little bracing up. Fresh air ought to be just the thing. And—let's leave that here, shall we?" he added, twitching the shawl away from the indignant sheriff's hands and bestowing it on his own side of the seat; and forestalled Royal's protest with, "Really, Sheriff. I'm sure Mrs. Meade would say it was questionable taste for morning wear — especially for a man of your age."

He steered the sputtering sheriff down the aisle of the car and out at the door, and it closed behind them.

Randall and Charity watched them go, both smiling a little, and when the two men had disappeared they sat quietly for a few moments. There were only one or two other people in the carriage, so they were nearly alone.

Randall gently turned over Charity's hand in his own, looking at the faint purple shadow of a bruise on her wrist. He looked down into her face. "You're sure you're all right, darling?" he said.

"Yes," said Charity. "They were a little bit rough with me, but — I'm not hurt. I'm fine now."

He smiled down at her, and leaned his head tiredly against the cushion of the seat, without taking his eyes from her face. The marks of two sleepless nights, and the days of anxiety, showed plainly on his face in the strong daylight.

"Poor darling," said Charity softly, touching his arm gently with her free hand. There was happiness, though, too, in her eyes as they dwelt on his tired face; a quiet joy in knowing that she was loved so much as to cause this concern. "Did I frighten you very much?"

Randall tried to laugh, not succeeding too well. "Frightened hardly seems like a big enough word."

Charity was looking down as she spoke, a little carefully. "Were you...afraid that the things they said about me were true?"

Randall moved his head awkwardly against the cushion, and stared across at a ray of sunlight on the opposite seat as he tried to think of the right words for his answer. "No," he said after a moment. "Never all the way. I didn't realize it then...but I know now that I didn't really believe it. But I was surely scared for a while, because the more I thought, the more I realized that I didn't know anything about you that could prove it all wrong. Nothing! Charity, do you realize that I don't even know your middle name?"

"I can remedy that easily enough," said Charity, gravely, but with a delightful little glimmering of humor in her voice. "I can tell you all sorts of things, in fact. What more about me would you like to know?"

"Everything," said Randall impulsively. "Everything there is to know. I want to know all about you—every last, littlest detail, so I'll have that many more things to love you for."

"And where shall I begin?" said Charity softly, her cheek against his arm.

"Don't begin now," said Randall. "You don't have to. The nicest thing is, I've got all the time in the world to learn."

* * *

"May I help you, Mrs. Meade?"

Mrs. Meade looked up from an assortment of yard goods that she had been sorting her way through for the past quarter of an hour without any apparent object. "Oh, no, thank you, Mr. Benton," she said rather abstractedly. "Thank you, I'm only looking about." She gave him a pleasant nod and a smile and turned to the next table.

The storekeeper could not help wondering, as he returned to his counter, exactly what it was that Mrs. Meade was looking for, since by this time she had

looked over nearly every display in the store. Whatever the object of her search, she did not seem particularly satisfied with the results, yet neither did she
seem impatient, for she was the last customer of the
evening, and showed no inclination towards leaving
any time soon.

The deeply colored sunset, the same that cast its
rays over Denver in the hour that Edgerton and his
companions were traversing that narrow street, was
streaming into the shop, its red glow falling over the
displays as if the windows had been tinted with blood.
The aroma of supper cooking drifted out from the living quarters at the back of the store, hovering around
the counter where Benton was going over the day's
accounts and hoping that Mrs. Meade would find
whatever it was she wanted before the meal was ready.
Older ladies always did take such time making up
their minds.

Mrs. Meade was frowning at a hurricane lamp
with a hopefully positioned price tag, displaying the
original price prominently crossed out and a more
attractive one substituted, when a series of thuds
overhead and a thunder of footsteps down the stairs
from the second floor made her turn, in time to see the
young deputy sheriff stumble down the last of the
stairs and make for the front door.

"Is something wrong, Richard?" called Mrs.
Meade.

"It's Miss Lewis—she's been taken ill. I've got
to go for a doctor." And he jerked the door open,
tripped over his own feet and then again over the
threshold, and somehow managed to get out of the
store and, it is devoutly to be hoped, down the outside
steps without further catastrophe.

Mrs. Meade did not wait to see, however, nor did she return to her shopping, but crossed the store to the staircase and ascended. Quietly she opened the door to the seamstress' room.

Diana Lewis did not look ill. She was by the mannequin at the other end of the room, her head bent slightly and her mouth a sharp, set line, working away at the white dress as if her life depended upon it. Mrs. Meade watched her for a moment, and then she stepped into the room and closed the door behind her.

Diana Lewis whipped round with a startled gasp. She stood staring at Mrs. Meade, one hand clenched and her thin body rigid.

"No, Miss Lewis," said Mrs. Meade firmly, "I'm afraid it won't do."

* * *

So the next morning when Edgerton and Andrew Royal, having come directly from the railway station, mounted the stairs and opened the door, they both halted momentarily and blinked in surprise at finding a tableau almost exactly like the one they had left—Diana Lewis seated on the sofa, and Mrs. Meade ensconced in an armchair, looking thoroughly mistress of the situation. The only new element was Royal's young deputy, who sat on a chair over near the sewing-table with a guilty, mortified expression on his boyish face.

"Now, before you say anything, Andrew, you must understand that it was not Richard's fault," said Mrs. Meade. "Anyone might have been taken in. *You* might if you had been the one to stay with her. She *was* an actress once, as she told us, and I have no doubt a very convincing one, too."

"What, do you mean she made an attempt at escape?" said Edgerton.

"Oh, yes. I thought she would. But since I was expecting it, I was able to be here and prevent it."

"*Expecting* it?"

"Yes," said Mrs. Meade. "You see, I never believed for a moment that a woman who could cold-bloodedly arrange for another girl to be murdered would give up those pearls so easily. Fear couldn't drive a woman to do such a thing, but greed might. That story she told us yesterday was, if you'll pardon the expression, so much hogwash. Oh, I've no doubt those people who abducted Charity were as vicious as she said—but surely, if she was clever enough to fashion this scheme she could have thought of a way to give them what they wanted and still make her own escape. *But she didn't want to give them the pearls.* That was clear all along. Those letters—the letters left in Charity's room—they were the most telling thing. They were intended to convince *us* that Charity was Mary Taylor. Remember that third letter that Diana Lewis wrote herself? That was to create the impression of *flight*. Why do that, if she expected Charity to be returned unharmed—and to establish her identity? No, what she really wanted was for Mary Taylor to be dead, so Diana Lewis could move quietly away to enjoy the profits of her robbery."

Edgerton seemed to have a suspicion of what was coming. "Then the pearls...on the shawl..."

"They were false, of course. Meant to deceive both us *and* the kidnappers. She hid the real ones here, in a place no one would ever think of looking for them, intending to collect them and make her departure when it was convenient. Her identity being found out yesterday was a blow, but she still thought she had a chance. While you were gone she feigned illness, alarmingly enough to send Richard rushing for a doctor — timing it for the moment when the Bentons would be at supper and the evening train for the west just about to depart. But as I said, I rather expected she would try, so I made a point of lingering in the store yesterday afternoon, and — well — "

Mrs. Meade finished with a quaint, half-embarrassed smile, as if to intimate that she could not think of anything more to add.

"You wouldn't happen to know," said Edgerton, "where the pearls *are* — would you, Mrs. Meade?"

Mrs. Meade rose from her chair. "Come over here, Mr. Edgerton, and I'll show you."

Edgerton laid the silk shawl, which he had carried with him from the train, across the sewing-table and followed her. Andrew Royal, his mouth open under a limp moustache, looked at the shawl with an expression of utter betrayal.

Mrs. Meade drew near the mannequin and extended her hand to touch the white dress. "Look at the pearl beading on the yoke. She always did such exquisite embroidery," she said reminiscently, "especially with beading. The pearls are all there — *on Charity's wedding-dress* — and they've been there all the time."

THE

PARTING GLASS

And all I've done for want of wit
To memory now I can't recall...

~ *"The Parting Glass" (traditional)*

It was afternoon, and the upper floor of the Colonial Hotel was still. Mrs. Meade sat in a rocking-chair in the square of sunlight that fell through her bedroom window, reading and rocking gently back and forth.

Mrs. Meade's migration to the Colonial was temporary, and had occurred on short notice. Two weeks before, her landlady, Mrs. Henney, had received word that her sister in Boulder was ill and required her presence. Mrs. Henney had no time to find someone who could run her little boarding-house satisfactorily in her absence, so she had decided to close it up, her ladies and gentleman consenting to be thrown on the hospitality of other establishments or friends for a week or two. Several of them had seen Mrs. Henney off at the station, even more flustered and near-hysterical than usual, laden with shawls, bonnet, carpetbag, parcels, umbrella — everything, in fact, but a pair of snowshoes — and finally, in a burst of tearful magnanimity as the train was about to pull out, offering to refund their rent for the days they would be in exile.

Mrs. Meade had therefore taken up residence at the Colonial Hotel, where she found much to interest her. Being a woman who all her life had found enjoyment in observing and interacting with people, she made the most of her opportunities for such in the company of the summer boarders and travelers who gathered around the dinner-tables at the Colonial. She had made several new friends, her room was neat, clean and convenient, and altogether her stay was less an exile than a pleasant interlude.

As Mrs. Meade turned over a page in her book, the silence was broken by three light muffled taps, as though at another door in the upstairs hallway. Mrs. Meade lifted her head and listened for a moment, but there was no further sound, so she dismissed it from her mind and returned her attention to her reading. The only sound to be heard in the room was the faint hum of insects from outdoors, and the blundering of one persistent fly around the top of the window.

Then suddenly there was an outburst of noises from beyond the closed door — somewhere just across the hall the bang of a door against a wall, a woman's shriek, and a man's loud angry voice mixed with a series of confused bumps and thuds. Mrs. Meade dropped her book and rose quickly. The whole floor of the hotel had come alive in a moment, with the sounds of doors opening and people's footsteps and questioning voices in the corridors.

There was already a knot of people in the
hallway when Mrs. Meade opened her door, but she
was still able to catch a distinct glimpse of what had
caused the disturbance. The door of the room immediately opposite hers was open, and in the middle
of the room a short, stocky, black-moustached man in
an overcoat had hold of the collar of a much taller
young man, who appeared somewhat dazed and confused, and was shaking and cuffing him vigorously.
Behind them on the edge of the bed, shrinking back
against the headboard as if she had been pushed or
had stumbled and fallen there, was a fair-haired young
girl.

"You young scoundrel!" exclaimed the stocky
man, with another indignant jerk. "You drunken
young cuss, I'll learn *you* to insult a lady! Get along,
there! Move!"

He alternately pushed and dragged the young
man through the door into the hall, where he was immediately assisted by the hands of several other people
who had no idea what they were helping with, but
were no less eager to help than if they had. The two of
them were borne away down the hall in a crowd. In the
commotion Mrs. Meade slipped from her doorway and
crossed into the other room, where the girl leaning
back limply at the head of the bed seemed to have been
almost forgotten.

"Are you all right, my dear?" she asked,
bending to lay a hand on her shoulder.

The girl looked up at her, and though her fair
face seemed blank and uncomprehending, Mrs. Meade
thought she saw a brief look of sharp distress in her
dull-blue eyes, as if they felt and expressed something
independent of the rest of her.

"Yes," she said after a few seconds. "Yes, I'm fine."

"Is there anything I can do for you?" said Mrs. Meade gently.

The girl, her eyes now fixed on the quilt, shook her head. "No, thank you...I'd just rather — be left alone."

She put her hand up over her mouth, but Mrs. Meade observed that it did not shake. Adept at discerning when another's presence was beneficial and when it was not necessary, she decided that in this case the girl probably *would* be better off left alone. So she exited the room with the same unobtrusive efficiency with which she had entered, and closed the door behind her.

She was not too reluctant to go, either, for her curiosity was tending in another direction. She had recognized the young man who had been one of the other principal performers in the chaotic scene just enacted, and she was very much interested in finding out just what had happened.

By the time she got downstairs, she found that the energetic black-haired man, along with a few other public-spirited volunteers, had already hustled the young man out of the hotel and off to the sheriff's office. The lobby and sitting-room were filled with buzzing little groups of people discussing the incident. Mrs. Meade listened here and listened there, inconspicuously, without taking part in the conversations. She was present when one of the men returned a quarter of an hour later and reported what had happened at the sheriff's. Then she went back upstairs to her own room, absently picked up the book she had let fall to the floor and placed it on the night-table, and sat down in her rocking-chair to think.

* * *

    She knew Clyde Renfrew quite well; his parents, both dead now, had been her friends. Clyde was a sober, steady young cattleman who lived some distance out of Sour Springs, coming into town occasionally to buy supplies or to arrange for the sale and shipment of his livestock. His serious, somewhat methodical manner of speaking and acting belied the fact that he had both brains and business sense — he had never been cheated. He was a bachelor still at twenty-five, known to be painfully shy of women. Local wits said it would probably take him a year or two to get up the nerve to speak to a woman, let alone propose marriage to her, and the eligible young ladies were all snapped up by more enterprising suitors before he could get fairly started. At any rate, he treated all women with scrupulous deference, did not speak to them if he could help it, and turned brick-red if cornered by one or trapped into conversation with a particularly lively specimen.

    There had been no notable departure from this behavior observed since his introduction to Dorene Leighton, but then again, Dorene was not of the type of girl whom Clyde usually found occasion to avoid.

    Dorene had come to Colorado with her aunt for her health, or for her aunt's health; nobody quite knew which. The aunt, Miss Asher, dominated any conversation where both were present, and nobody had the chance to learn much about Dorene at all. A small, timid-looking girl of about twenty, she wore pale colors that made her appear to be continually on the point of fading away altogether, and her fair hair was cut in a bang across her forehead like a much younger girl's. When one had the chance to hear her speak, her low voice had a pleasing musical quality, but this chance did not come often.

Dorene had come into contact with Clyde Renfrew through mutual friends, a family in Sour Springs whose acquaintance she and her aunt had made early in their stay. They had been in each other's company at a few picnics and dinners, and Clyde had called at the Coopers' once or twice when Dorene happened to be spending the day with them. By all accounts he had behaved towards her with the same studious politeness that he showed all women, but they had seemed to appreciate each other's company in a reserved way.

On this particular afternoon, Clyde had called at the Colonial Hotel at about a quarter to two, and asked the clerk for the number of Miss Leighton's room. He had gone upstairs, and nothing more was seen or heard of him for the better part of an hour.

Around ten minutes to three, the man who had the room next to Dorene Leighton's—a traveling patent-medicine salesman named Hollister—had heard muffled voices through the wall, and then a woman's cry of alarm or distress. He had immediately rushed out of his room, burst open the door of the next one and found Dorene Leighton struggling in Clyde Renfrew's embrace as he forcibly attempted to kiss her. Hollister had "broken it up," to use his own expression, by which time other witnesses had arrived. Clyde was evidently drunk; there was liquor on his breath, he was unsteady on his feet and could not speak clearly. Hollister, as well as one or two others who had been in the doorway, said there had been an empty glass decanter on the bureau in the room, which the hotel chambermaid insisted was mostly full earlier in the day when she did the rooms.

They dragged Clyde down to the sheriff's office, where by a combination of bullying and black coffee he was got into a condition for questioning. But even so they did not glean anything of significance. Clyde said that Miss Leighton had asked him to call on her at the hotel; he confusedly admitted to having had a drink, but claimed he could remember nothing of what had happened afterward. Sheriff Royal had locked him up on a charge of assault and one of being drunk and disorderly, had pacified the red-hot Hollister and shooed everybody out of his office, and there the case stood.

Mrs. Meade rocked slowly back and forth in her chair. She was profoundly puzzled. There were the facts, and they seemed undeniable, but the story shocked her to a great degree. *Clyde?* Clyde Renfrew, of all people, drunkenly insulting a woman? She would have thought him the very last person likely to do such a thing. So, apparently, would most of the other people she had overheard discussing the matter in the lobby. Surprise, puzzlement, incredulity had been the prevailing sentiments among them. More than once she had heard a near-echo of her own thought: "But *Clyde?* I'd never have expected — "

What could possibly have happened to him?

Mrs. Meade shook her head. She could not rid herself of the idea that there must be an explanation somewhere — that there had been some kind of misconception or mistake.

* * *

At half-past three, Miss Asher entered the hotel and sailed majestically up the stairs to her niece's room, her lips pinched firmly together in a manner that signified disapproval, having been informed by someone in the street as to what had occurred. Miss Asher was a tall, substantial woman, with gray hair dressed in innumerable little tight curls, a fountain of rather bluish-colored lace spilling over the bosom of her lavender silk dress and a masterpiece of a large feathered hat to top it all, and the combined effect when she turned a corner at top speed was a *swish* that made anyone in her path fall back feeling as if an ocean wave had gone over them. She turned the corner into her niece's room with just such a *swish*, the expression on her face boding no good, and the door closed firmly behind her.

Mrs. Meade, who had learned from the afternoon's occurrences that one must leave one's door ajar if one is to remain apprised of events, had arranged herself in her rocking-chair, decorously faced at an angle away from the door, but one which still allowed her to see and hear quite well through the three inches' opening at which she had set it. She had a glimpse of lavender silk and foreboding expression, and after Miss Asher had shut her niece's door was able to listen to the tenor, if not the words, of the conversation that took place behind it. Miss Asher was an orator among women, whose voice rung with feeling and italics. For a space of about ten minutes Mrs. Meade listened to her voice rising and falling, with occasionally what sounded like a faint protest from Dorene, and then after Miss Asher had wound down, a few minutes of unhappy silence. At some point during this interval Miss Asher evidently rang for the chambermaid, who presently climbed the stairs and knocked at the door. Miss Asher appeared briefly and presented her with a severely folded little note, with the instructions, "See that this is delivered to the sheriff at once."

Consequently, in a little while Sheriff Andrew Royal came climbing up the stairs and stopped at the door — looking, in the brief glimpse Mrs. Meade had of him, as if he did not relish his errand any too well — and knocked. He was admitted, and a second conference took place behind the closed door. Miss Asher's voice was more modulated in the presence of a third party, but she possessed the faculty of talking smoothly over anyone who attempted to remonstrate, so Mrs. Meade guessed that she had it very much her own way. Dorene seemed to try and interrupt anxiously once or twice, but was not allowed to succeed, and Sheriff Royal did not seem to be allowed to even finish a sentence.

In about ten minutes he came out, bidding a rather grim good-afternoon, and once the door was safely closed behind him he gave a snort that was not meant for anyone else's ears and stomped off down the stairs. Mrs. Meade arose from her chair, and went out into the hall and followed him down.

As she reached the turn at the landing a door opened on the floor above, and Miss Asher's voice came clearly down to her: "Do not be an idiot, Dorene. If we did not seek reparation there would be Things Said, and I shall never have Things Said about any niece in my charge." Whereupon the door closed uncompromisingly.

Mrs. Meade came quickly down the lower flight

of stairs just as the broad-shouldered, ungainly figure of the gray-haired sheriff was leaving the foot of them.

"Andrew," she said.

Sheriff Royal turned abruptly to look up. "Oh, it's you," he said as she came down and joined him; a greeting which sounded rather ungracious, but which did not seem to bother Mrs. Meade in the least.

"Andrew, could I speak to you for a moment?" she asked.

Royal glanced around and motioned with the battered hat in his hand toward the hotel's small best parlor off the lobby, which was empty. They went toward it together. The harassed expression on the sheriff's face as he stalked beside her, coupled with a somewhat hunted look in his eye, made Mrs. Meade feel sure he was only waiting till he had reached suitable surroundings to explode. As soon as she had closed the parlor door, he did so.

"Women!" he snorted. "If there's anything worse than having a woman after you, it's getting between two of them."

"Then perhaps I should not make matters worse by making a third," said Mrs. Meade, with a slight twitch about her mouth that belied the matter-of-fact tone of the suggestion.

Royal waved it away with his hat. "Oh, you don't count. That is, I mean—" He strove to extricate himself from this linguistic tangle, and compromised with, "Well, you're a different breed from that Asher woman, thank goodness."

"I should not repeat this in public, but I consider that a very nice compliment," Mrs. Meade told him kindly, and the sheriff harrumphed and waved that away too. "What has Miss Asher done?"

"It's not so much what she's done," said Royal. "It's the way she goes about it. She talks like she's the only person who knows how to do things properly and if you don't do just what she says you're not even worth bowing to on the street." He stopped for breath, and added, "She wants to sue young Renfrew for damages."

"She does — or her niece does?"

"She does all the talking for her niece," said Andrew Royal grimly. "The girl would rather try and forget about the whole thing, to my mind, but Aunt Asher is boss. To hear her talk you'd think she'd like to go after him herself with a horsewhip. But at least she's agreed to settle it out of court — easier on everybody's feelings."

"Will Clyde settle, do you think?" said Mrs. Meade.

"He's got no choice," said Royal, looking at her as though a little surprised by the question.

"I simply can't understand it," said Mrs. Meade. "Clyde was such a nice upstanding boy. I knew his mother very well, and she was always so proud of him — I can't think what can have happened."

"Hmmm…well," said Royal. "How much do you know about it?"

"As much as anyone else in Sour Springs does just now," said Mrs. Meade, and the sheriff grunted in dry appreciation. "Perhaps a little more, since I was nearby when it happened. My room is just across the hall from Dorene Leighton's, in fact."

"You seem to have a knack for being just across the hall when things happen," said Sheriff Royal, eyeing her. "But this isn't like that Bradford affair, where it all happened at night and all we had to go on were things we found. Plenty of people around to see and hear this time."

"Yes," said Mrs. Meade, "but—what about Clyde? Did he tell you anything—try to explain, or to defend himself at all?"

Royal shook his head. "Nope. Took us a few minutes to get him sobered up enough to talk—funny thing, I've never heard of him being drunk before, but there's no doubt about it, he was soused. Then when they told him what he'd done he pretty near turned green—I thought he was going to slide right off his chair. But all he'd say was that he couldn't remember anything."

"That was your first mistake, then," said Mrs. Meade, "letting them *tell* him what had happened instead of waiting to hear him speak first. He was in no condition then to know what was true and what wasn't."

Andrew Royal stared at her for a moment, as if a new idea was just filtering into his brain. "You don't mean to tell me you don't *believe* it?"

"I did not tell you anything of the kind," said Mrs. Meade firmly. "I merely think you have forfeited your only chance of getting a clear account of the incident—of Clyde's version of it, at least."

"How many versions d'you think there are?" growled Royal (a not entirely serious question).

"Four, at least," was Mrs. Meade's entirely unexpected answer; and then after a second she added, "perhaps five."

Royal did not attempt to reply for a minute. "Oh," he said at last, just a little sarcastically, scratching the back of his head with the hand that still held his hat. "Five."

He cleared his throat ferociously, a habit of his when he was at a loss and did not want anyone else to know it. "Guess I'd better get back to the office," he said. "Anything else I can do for you, Mrs. Meade?"

"No," said Mrs. Meade a trifle absently, having become rather thoughtful in the brief interval; "no, not just at present."

Royal stared for a second, and then he clapped his hat on crooked and made his escape.

* * *

"It is shocking," said Miss Powers warmly, "quite shocking."

Miss Powers, small and sheeplike, had a soft, mellow voice with a little vibration in it that lent the impression of heartfelt feeling to everything she said. She also had not an original idea in her head, but she possessed the gift of absorbing the opinions of the company about her and repeating them warmly as if they were her own. People often liked her very much for the first day or two that they knew her, until it began to be borne in upon them that Miss Powers was merely a glorified echo.

Miss Asher, however, found Miss Powers' earnest concurrence very gratifying. She agreed grimly in her turn. "And it all might easily have been averted," she said. "It was never *my* wish that Dorene should be introduced to that young man. From the very first I considered him a most undesirable acquaintance."

"I'm sure you were right," said Miss Powers feelingly. "And yet he always *acted* rather like a gentleman, I suppose."

"Gen'lman my foot," said Mr. Hollister, who was consuming a hearty meal a little further down the table, leaning forward over his plate with his napkin tucked into his collar. "A right-down young scoundrel what don't deserve to be called any better, 's what he is. But I told 'im. I give 'im a piece of my mind."

A doubly large mouthful of food stopped up any further remarks from the commercial gentleman, whose experiences had certainly not impaired his appetite. Miss Asher looked down the table at him with a faint air of distaste. She inclined her head slightly as though forced to agree with him, but against her will. It appeared that being under obligation to Mr. Hollister, a person of whom she had no opinion, was the part she liked least of the whole affair.

"I had spoken to Dorene more than once about him, but to no avail," she observed, returning to her dinner and the mutually agreeable society of Miss Powers. "I cannot tell you how this has distressed and grieved me. I have always endeavored to do my Duty by her, but really sometimes Dorene is a Sad Trial to me."

"I wouldn't have thought that," observed Miss Brewster, a straight, thin woman who spoke in jerks like throwing darts.

"One would never guess it by your fortitude, Miss Asher," said Miss Powers, sympathetically misinterpreting.

Miss Asher allowed herself a grenadierly simper. She took another spoonful of soup, and then sighed. "The trouble with Dorene is not so much rebelliousness, as a Lack of Understanding. I often tell her things again and again, but she simply does not seem to comprehend them. And This is the result."

Miss Asher and Miss Powers both shook their heads regretfully. Miss Brewster merely said "Hm!"

"What a respectable assemblage of ghouls we are!" murmured Mrs. Clairborn to Mrs. Meade, under cover of the discussion. Mrs. Clairborn was a well-to-do summer traveler, an elegant, humorous woman whom Mrs. Meade found excellent company. "Don't ever tell me that genteel old ladies dislike scandal. They're all enjoying it to the hilt — even Miss Asher. One would think she would have a little more feeling for her niece, and not just her own position."

"Poor Dorene!" said her daughter Phyllis, a warm-hearted, brown-eyed girl of twenty, from the other corner of the table, where she sat at Mrs. Meade's left. "I think she liked him, you know. She didn't say anything — she doesn't say anything about *anything*, really — but I saw her looking at him once or twice, and she looked quite miserable."

"Miserable?" queried Mrs. Meade, to whom the adjective was unexpected.

"Oh, yes. Dorene always looks haunted when she's trying to make up her mind about something, even if it's only which kind of sandwich to take at luncheon."

Mrs. Clairborn raised her fine arched eyebrows and shook her head, her small jet earrings swinging. "Well, according to Miss Asher's august judgment, she made a wrong selection this once."

"So it would seem," said Mrs. Meade.

"Yes," agreed Phyllis. "It's too bad. Isn't it a shame that people always turn out to be different than you think them?"

Mrs. Meade looked for a second at the girl's honest, sympathetic young face. "Yes," she said, "I should think that is one of the greatest shames there is in the world."

* * *

The morning air was cool and fresh. Above the town, the mountains stood crisp against the clear sky, their snow-streaked crests looking almost near enough to touch. Sheriff Royal strode along the boardwalk, upon which the early morning sun was pouring brightly down through gaps in the trees, his much-worn boots thumping on the wide weathered planks. Occasionally he met a lady walking in the opposite direction and gave her a short nod of greeting, but without paying any particular attention to her. Therefore Mrs. Meade saw him well before he saw her, even though she had been walking along rather deep in thought herself. She considered for a moment, and then quickened her steps slightly to join him.

Royal had stopped to look into the window of the harness shop when Mrs. Meade came up to him. "Good morning, Andrew," she said.

"Oh—good morning," he said, looking round, and pushed his hat back a little by way of courtesy.

"I was out doing a few errands," said Mrs. Meade briskly, glancing down at the reticule on her arm, "but I'm rather glad I met you. I have been doing a good deal of thinking since last night, and...I have a slightly unusual favor to ask of you, I think."

Sheriff Royal looked slightly alarmed, but signified his willingness to listen to her request.

"Would you let me come and talk to Clyde for a few minutes? I don't know if it will do him any good, or even do me any good, but I feel somehow that I must understand this affair better, even if — even if it's only a sad truth after all," she concluded with a little sigh.

"You've been thinking again!" accused Andrew Royal, rather unnecessarily. "You still won't believe he did it, will you. How *can't* you?"

Mrs. Meade shook her head. "No, Andrew, I can't say for certain I don't believe it. I honestly don't know what to think. It just seems so *wrong*, somehow."

"Instinct!" growled Royal. "You can't judge everything on instinct, Mrs. Meade. No matter how wrong it looks, the fact — "

"The fact is, there may be more than one possible explanation for a set of facts, and the most obvious one that everyone seizes upon needn't be it."

Royal was shaking his head back and forth. "I don't know what you're getting at, but there's one fact you can't get round — an eyewitness."

"Ah, but can't you?" said Mrs. Meade. "You remember I said yesterday that there were five different versions of the story — versions told by five different people. Clyde Renfrew, Dorene Leighton, Mr. Hollister, myself, and — Miss Asher, perhaps. Each can tell you what they saw, and heard, and were told, and each version will be a little different."

"But they all saw and heard the same stuff," said Royal.

Mrs. Meade shook her head. "But each may have *thought* they were seeing something different."

"Hey?"

"Mr. Hollister," said Mrs. Meade, "from what I have seen of him at the dinner table these past few weeks, is a brash, boisterous, headlong sort of person, the sort who is very likely to jump to conclusions.

Suppose it this way for just a moment: Mr. Hollister is in his room. He hears voices in the next room — agitated or disputing voices, perhaps. He knows the next room belongs to a young lady, but one of the voices is a man's voice — and he immediately jumps to the conclusion that the man is an unwelcome intruder. He rushes out into the hall and bursts unceremoniously into the room to catch a glimpse of Clyde standing close to Dorene — perhaps with his arms around her — and Dorene, a timid girl under any circumstances, could easily have been startled into screaming by Mr. Hollister's plunge into the room, especially if it was already a fraught moment. Mr. Hollister could have interrupted any number of things, from the reconciliation of a quarrel, to an awkward declaration of love, or even a proposal of marriage — "

Andrew Royal gave a short bark of a laugh. "Clyde? Proposing marriage?" He recollected himself and became gruffly serious again. "Go on."

"Any of those things," resumed Mrs. Meade, "but Mr. Hollister leaped to the conclusion that it was an insult he witnessed. Later on, Dorene could have simply been too embarrassed and ashamed to contradict him with the truth."

"Hmmm...well," said Andrew Royal. He looked somewhat embarrassed himself. He cleared his throat vigorously. "It's another way to look at it, but — hem! — don't you think it's — not exactly — "

Mrs. Meade also cleared her throat, but delicately. "You mean that the theory of a willing embrace is — hardly more creditable to either of them, under the circumstances?"

Andrew Royal's face turned a shade redder, and his expression admitted his answer in the affirmative.

"I would have always expected it of Clyde to be scrupulous," said Mrs. Meade; "I'd hardly have thought he would choose such an improper time and place for a declaration, if not for the fact that—"

"The fact that he'd had a couple," Royal filled in, blunt in his turn. "And that *is* a fact."

"And that's one of the things I don't understand," said Mrs. Meade with another sigh.

"Well...look at it your way, maybe it does make sense. Maybe he had a couple of drinks because he was trying to get up the nerve to say something to her."

"It needn't follow, though, that a careful, reasoning sort of man like Clyde would choose one of the most important moments in his life to do something so contrary to his usual character. Oh, Andrew, this endless speculation isn't doing us a bit of good. We'll never get anywhere if we don't *do* something."

Sheriff Royal looked somewhat taken aback by this declaration. He had, it was true, a respect for Mrs. Meade's insight that she had well earned, but he had not yet accustomed himself to the unexpectedness of her thought processes.

He started to open his mouth in what was clearly going to be an expression of outrage or a protest, but Mrs. Meade read his mind, and raised a reassuring hand to forestall him. "Now, that's not what I mean, Andrew. You won't have to do anything strenuous, and it doesn't involve Miss Asher. What I *meant* to say is, we'll never know anything unless we have some help from Clyde. May I see him?"

"Don't see anything wrong with it," said Royal, knitting his bushy brows to think it over. "You could walk down with me to the jail now, if you don't mind that. I can't take him out to see you, not without having Aunt Asher ambush me, that is. All right with you?"

"Certainly," said Mrs. Meade.

Sheriff Royal made way for her to pass him on the boardwalk, and then fell into step beside her as they walked back down the street.

* * *

Mrs. Meade sat in a chair in the sheriff's office, her gloved hands folded over her reticule in her lap, and observed Clyde Renfrew with grave attention. He was a big young man, with light hair and a face that was usually serious but still expressed natural good-nature. Now, though, his entire attitude spoke dejection; his shoulders slumped dispiritedly and he could hardly lift his eyes from the floor.

He had looked somewhat surprised to see Mrs. Meade when Sheriff Royal brought him out from the back of the jail into the office, but did not seem able to bring himself to speak even to ask her why she was there. So Mrs. Meade, who was very good at reading unspoken questions, broke the silence by answering his very simply: "I did not want you to think all your friends had deserted you."

Clyde looked up for a second, and then down at the floor again. "Well," he said in a lifeless voice, "I wouldn't blame them if they did."

"Now, that does not seem a very promising attitude to take," said Mrs. Meade.

Clyde said nothing.

A feeling of pity overmastered whatever else Mrs. Meade might have been thinking, and she impulsively leaned forward and laid her hand on his arm. "Clyde, I am not so ready to dismiss you as you think. I've known you a good many years, and I knew your father and mother. I've never thought you would be the kind of young man to insult a woman, even if you were—were not quite yourself."

"Up until yesterday, I'd have thought so too," said Clyde.

"Can you not remember anything of what happened? of how it came about? Anything at all?"

Clyde opened his mouth slowly, his brow knitting as if with thought. He looked across at her, and for the first time Mrs. Meade thought she caught a look of hesitancy in his eyes. He shut his mouth again, undecided.

But in the few seconds of silence Andrew Royal had suddenly tumbled to the point. "There *was* something you remember!" he said explosively, sitting up with a violent creak from his wooden swivel chair.

Mrs. Meade gave him a quick, inconspicuous shake of the head. It was too soon to press the point.

"Why don't you begin at the beginning, and tell me just what you can remember happening," she said to Clyde. "You said that Miss Leighton sent for you—is that correct?"

"Yes," said Clyde. He was still a little uncomfortable, but he seemed to relax somewhat as he spoke, his words gradually coming more freely. "She sent me a note. It said she wanted to ask my advice about a business matter—she asked me to come to the hotel because she knew her aunt was going to be out that afternoon, and it was something she couldn't talk about with her aunt there.

"I went to the hotel—I had to ask for her room number at the desk, because she hadn't put it in the note—I went upstairs and knocked at her door, and she let me in." A vague, troubled look came up in his eyes like a fog, as if he were back in that moment, seeing Dorene as she opened the door. He swallowed and went on. "She told me what she'd wanted to see me about. She said she had some money her grandfather'd left her, three or four years ago, but she'd given her aunt the control over it when she came of age, so as not to have the bother of dealing with it herself. But she felt differently now, because she couldn't touch it—her aunt wouldn't let her have the least bit to spend unless it was on something she approved of. Dor—Miss Leighton wanted to ask me what was the best way to get control of it herself again, without having too much of a fight with her aunt. I think—she kind of wanted a way to do it without telling her aunt at all."

He came to a halt for a moment, frowning, and rubbed his temple as if it hurt. Mrs. Meade noted the action.

"What did you do while you talked? Did you sit down?"

"She did, after a few minutes. In a chair. I might have—no, I think I walked up and down a little while I talked—maybe leaned against the wall by the bureau."

"And then?"

"There was a decanter full of sherry on the bureau, and some glasses. At some point while we were talking she stood up and asked me if I'd like a drink before I went, and poured a glass for me, and I took it."

"Did you have more than one glass?" said Mrs. Meade.

"Yes," said Andrew Royal before Clyde could

answer.

Clyde turned toward him with the first appearance of interest he had shown so far. "I did?"

"She says you did. Admitted it, anyway. Didn't seem to want to, but Aunt Asher bullied her into it."

"I suppose I must have, then," said Clyde wearily, relapsing into indifference.

Mrs. Meade leaned forward a little. "Do you remember pouring a drink for yourself at any time?"

"No-o-o…" Clyde sounded doubtful.

"And then what happened? How did your conversation end?"

"We were still talking about the money. I don't remember it ending—I just—" Clyde was floundering now, grasping vaguely for the memory. He shook his head. "There was a picture on the wall, wavering back and forth, like it was floating…I think I felt kind of sick. The next thing I remember is hearing somebody shouting at me, from a long ways off it seemed, and then Hollister was shaking me. I can't remember."

"The curious thing is," said Mrs. Meade, "you were upstairs for more than an hour, between the time you stopped at the desk and the time Mr. Hollister burst in. How can you account for all that time? How long did you discuss the question of Dorene's money?"

"I don't know," said Clyde, shaking his head again. "It couldn't have been that long, but I haven't got the least idea."

"If you say it wasn't that long, then you *have* got some idea," said Royal shortly. "How long did it take you to finish that first drink?"

"I don't know."

Royal got up impatiently. "You mean to tell me you had no idea of the time at all? You didn't look at your watch once? Or a clock?"

"Yes," said Mrs. Meade, "one should always be aware of the time, for one never knows when one may be called upon to produce an alibi."

Sheriff Royal coughed suddenly, but Clyde looked piteously rebuked.

"Leaving that aside for the moment," said Mrs. Meade, "I am, admittedly, not an expert in such matters, but—I suppose *two* glasses of sherry could have *had* such an effect upon you?"

"The decanter was practically empty afterwards," said Clyde, sinking back into his former state of despondence. "Hollister saw it; other people saw it. And about the only thing I *am* sure of is that it was mostly full when I went into the room. I must have just drunk more without remembering it."

"But you *don't* drink, ordinarily, do you?"

"Well, not as we know the meaning of the word," said Clyde. "I mean, if I'm trying to close a deal with a man and he's pushing to buy me a drink, I'll have one with him, but not more—do you see? And I've been known to have a glass of sherry if it's served at a dinner I'm invited to...not that I'm invited to dinners that often," he added with a gloom that seemed separate from the subject at hand.

"Then that was the reason you accepted the glass of sherry Dorene Leighton offered you—just politeness?"

A rather funny smile replaced the strained expression on Clyde's face, a smile that seemed both shy and tender. "Well—I don't know," he said awkwardly. "It was more the way she looked. She seemed like a—like a little girl playing at being hostess, and anxious to get it all right—the way she had the glasses set out so carefully, and tried to pronounce all her words just right when she asked me. I—I kind of felt I'd hurt her feelings if I said no."

"That is also why you accepted a second glass, perhaps?" suggested Mrs. Meade.

Clyde shook his head again and reverted to his old refrain. "I don't know."

"So, if you are not accustomed to much strong drink," said Mrs. Meade, "do you suppose the second glass might have affected you, so that you un-thinkingly drank more—for instance, if you were nervous, perhaps?"

"I—don't know what you mean," said Clyde, his eyes shifting away from hers.

Mrs. Meade deftly skirted the issue again. "Do you know Mr. Hollister?"

"No. I don't know him, but I've seen him around—he's been out working the town. I saw him in the saloon the other day, buying drinks all around and trying to fast-talk everybody into buying his toothache oil, or whatever it is."

"You met Dorene Leighton at a dinner at the Coopers', didn't you?" said Mrs. Meade incon-sequently, as though refreshing her memory on a minor point.

"No, a picnic," said Clyde. "But I did see her at a dinner once."

The way he said it made it sound as if every time he had seen Dorene was marked off as a sig-nificant occasion in his memory, a precious stone on a chain of plain days.

"There is one other thing," said Mrs. Meade. "My room is just across the hall from Dorene's. Yesterday afternoon, a few moments before Mr.

Hollister began shouting, I head three taps in succession, as if someone had rapped lightly on a door or a wall. Do you know anything about that?"

Clyde shrugged, with an air of bewilderment. "I've told you, I wasn't in any shape to tell whether I tapped on anything or not."

"If you were as intoxicated as we have all been led to believe," said Mrs. Meade decisively, "you would not have *tapped* on anything. You would have banged it, or at least thumped it."

Here they were interrupted by a recurrence of the sheriff's cough, which took a moment or two to bring under control this time. Clyde and Mrs. Meade looked at him, and he waved for them to go on, his face red and eyes watering with the effort.

Mrs. Meade decided it was time to abandon all form of pretense or subtlety. "Clyde," she said, "I wish you would give me your honest opinion—your opinion, mind, not your deductions—as to what took place yesterday afternoon. I know there is something you have been hesitating to say. If I were you I should say it, even if it is not something calculated to do you any good."

Clyde fidgeted for a moment, and then leaned forward in his chair to look entreatingly across at her as he spoke. "It isn't something I can get hold of," he said. "I don't know if it's just something I thought up myself—like something you dreamed, and then when you wake up you're not sure if it really happened or not. I just have this feeling that—*whatever* I did—if I ever did try to kiss her, or if I said something—tried to tell her—whatever it was, I just have a feeling that *she didn't object*, do you understand?"

Andrew Royal fell back a step, staring at him in

mixed astonishment and indignation. "Then why the devil didn't you ever *say* so?"

"Do you think I *would*?" demanded Clyde, returning the look.

Andrew Royal swung abruptly away and took a turn up and down the room, rubbing the back of his neck. Mrs. Meade could tell he was attempting to control his feelings, and correctly attributed this forbearance to the fact of her presence.

He turned just as abruptly and came back. "Now, listen," he said. "I can see what you're trying to do. But you stand to lose your character here, besides a decent amount of money, and you're going to let it go without saying even *that* to defend yourself?"

"Yes," said Clyde. "I am."

His face was set in a way that told Mrs. Meade he could be as stubbornly settled as a rock when he chose, and the badgering of a dozen Andrew Royals would not move him.

"I think I understand," she said. Clyde looked at her, and his glance fell somewhat confusedly from the gentle penetration in her own blue-gray eyes. "You were beginning to fall for her, weren't you."

He admitted it, in a very low husky tone. "I thought—that she liked me a little," he said, "and that—but it's no use now. I can never say anything to her; she'd only think worse of me."

"I would not be so sure of that," said Mrs. Meade. "Because there is just one thing that is certain — *Dorene knows the truth about what happened yesterday afternoon.*"

* * *

"Well," Royal admitted, after he had locked Clyde in the cell again and come back to see Mrs. Meade to the door, "I won't deny it, looks like you're right again. It's pretty clear to me—he's keeping his mouth shut to protect the girl's good name, and ruining his own while he's at it."

"Wouldn't any gentleman do the same?" said Mrs. Meade.

"Well...yes," said Royal, in a kind of indistinct growl. "But what burns me is that he *has* to. With anybody else he could have just apologized for losing his head and it'd have been forgot well enough—but not with Aunt Asher, oh, no!"

"But it still doesn't quite fit," said Mrs. Meade, shaking her head in impulsive dissatisfaction. "There's one thing I still can't account for. What about the three taps?"

"Three tap—oh, blast the three taps!" said Royal. "Who knows what they were. Probably was in some other room and didn't have anything to do with it at all."

"Perhaps," said Mrs. Meade, "but when I was sitting there in my rocking-chair yesterday afternoon, and heard them—without the least idea that anything was about to go wrong—my impression was that they came from across the hall. And yet that would mean something else entirely, wouldn't it?"

"What's eating you now?" said Royal inelegantly, putting his head on one side and squinting at her from under a bushy eyebrow. "Earlier you said you thought there was more to the story than folks figured. You've got what you wanted now; you've heard the rest. And you're not satisfied?"

"We've heard more of the story, yes," Mrs.

Meade corrected him, "but I believe we still have not heard the *whole* story. It can't be complete if there is something left out. And the three taps—"

"The three taps," said Royal under his breath. "Well, what about them?"

"Just this," said Mrs. Meade. "When two people are in a room together, what occasion would one of them have to rap on the door? Isn't that usually what happens just before someone is *admitted* to a room? Couldn't it mean that, for at least a part of that hour which is unaccounted for, either Clyde or Dorene was not in the room at all?"

Andrew Royal gave a groan rather like a long-suffering cow. "Mrs. Meade, have you got to make everything so complicated?"

Mrs. Meade started slightly, as if at something she was thinking. "Of course," she said half to herself. "That was it. I knew there was something odd."

"What was?"

"Did you notice—Clyde said that Dorene offered him a drink *before he went?* And yet it couldn't have been very far into the hour at all. *Did* he leave—? But no, that doesn't fit—" She was speaking to herself again, in fragments of half-formed thought, her forehead knit with perplexity.

"Sounds more like she wished he would leave," said the sheriff.

"Perhaps," said Mrs. Meade, "you are not so very far wrong."

She was thinking back—to a dinner-table conversation, an expression in Dorene Leighton's eyes, a murmur overheard through a door set ajar. She nodded her head slowly.

And then she quoted, unexpectedly, "'And all

the harm I've ever done, alas, it was to none but me...'"

"What?" said Andrew Royal, even more surprised than before.

"Nothing," said Mrs. Meade. "Nothing, only it seemed rather apt...for both of them, perhaps." She paused, and then spoke slowly. "Has it ever occurred to you, Andrew, that this entire incident may have been an elaborate production that someone has put on to cover up something very simple?"

"If that's what happened," said Royal, who had run out of objections, "then they've done a doggoned good job of it."

* * *

Miss Asher, a workbasket containing her embroidery in her hand, opened the door to her room. She paused on the threshold. Dorene was sitting by the window at the other side of the room, looking out of it. She did not move nor turn her head at her aunt's entrance, as if she had not even heard. She seemed a quiet, colorless shadow herself, sitting there in the late-afternoon shade.

Miss Asher closed the door. "There you are," she said. "I was looking for you."

Dorene looked down, and stretched out her folded hands on her lap, listlessly. "I was in my room," she said in a voice to match. "I heard Mrs. Meade come upstairs, a little while ago, and I thought that she might come over to see me. So I came in here." She looked out the window again. "I—didn't want to see her just then."

"That's just as well," said Miss Asher grimly.

She crossed to the bureau and put down her work-basket.

Dorene said, with a little difficulty, "She's — been very kind to me."

Miss Asher shot a sharp sideways glance at her. Dorene was still staring drearily out of the window. There was another moment of silence. Then as if the girl's silence itself had irritated her, Miss Asher turned to face her niece with impatience, but no abating of her own dignity. "You must stop this foolishness, Dorene. You will forget about it all soon enough."

"Will I?" It was spoken very low.

Miss Asher pressed her lips firmly together to restrain her irritation, and then after a moment she spoke again. "Sheriff Royal is coming here again to-morrow morning to settle about the money," she said. "You and I will see him together. And you will not make an exhibition of yourself as you did yesterday." Another pause. "You *know* that you have no other choice, Dorene."

Dorene did not answer. Miss Asher gave her another look of disapproval, and then turned back to the bureau and opened a drawer.

* * *

When Mr. Hollister, his clinking sample case in his hand, climbed the stairs that afternoon and pushed open the door to his room, he halted for a second in understandable surprise at the spectacle within — that of a genteel-looking middle-aged lady standing near a chair with her hand just stretched out to touch the heavy gray overcoat draped over the back of it, an almost comical expression of alarm and dismay on her face.

"Oh *dear* me," exclaimed the lady, regarding the newcomer with a flustered and apologetic manner. "I am terribly sorry—you must pardon me, Mr. Hollister; I believe I must have entered the wrong room. I came up to see Miss Leighton, you see, but I must have gone past her door and opened the wrong one. I had thought she was out, until I saw your coat on the chair here just now, and realized my mistake." She advanced to meet him, with her hands clasped in a rather helpless manner and an abashed half-smile. "You will forgive me, I hope, Mr. Hollister?"

"Why, certainly, ma'am," said Hollister, taking off his hat from the top and making a little bow, in one glib motion on which he rather prided himself. "Nothing like an honest mistake, is what I always say."

"I really can't think how I came to make it! I suppose I must have misread the number on the door—I'm afraid my eyes are not what they once were."

Hollister scented a professional opportunity. "Do you get pain in 'em regularly, ma'am?"

"Well, not *regularly*," said Mrs. Meade, adapting herself to the situation, "but sometimes—"

That was all the encouragement Hollister needed. "Then let me introduce to you," he said, putting his sample case down on the bureau and beginning to energetically undo the buckles, "the re*mark*able qualities of Pollard's Proven Remedial Tonic. It might be just the thing you need. You'll go a long way before you find anything as helpful as Pollard's Proven, ma'am. Its remarkable remedial qualities have caused comment from coast to coast."

"Have they really?" said Mrs. Meade, looking

appropriately intrigued.

"Oh, yes; yes indeed." He had been extracting a number of small identical black medicine bottles from the case, and set them up in a row along the edge of the bureau with the labels outward as if to create the impression of a shelf in a druggist's window. "Pollard's Proven is your resort for just about anything that may be wrong with you, ma'am. It relieves headache, earache, toothache, back-ache, throat-ache, congestion, inflammation, and cold-in-the-head."

"Dear me, it must be powerful," said Mrs. Meade.

"It is that, ma'am. Powerful's an excellent choice of words, ma'am." Mr. Hollister spoke so feelingly, it was evident he had never had such an understanding and appreciative potential customer. "It may be just the thing what'll help you with your eyesight."

Mrs. Meade did not inquire which of Pollard's Proven Remedial Qualities would be able to do that, which undoubtedly raised her another point in the commercial gentleman's favor. Mr. Hollister had arranged himself smilingly beside his merchandise with his hand resting on the bureau, looking like he was posing for a photograph which would be handed down to posterity, so perhaps making any intelligent remark without betraying her state of mind was beyond her just then.

She retreated into her prior apologetic manner. "I feel I ought to buy a bottle, just to make up for the trouble I've given you, Mr. Hollister!"

"Oh, it's no—I mean, don't let that be your reason, ma'am," said Hollister, catching himself on the brink of repudiating a sale. "Let Pollard's Proven speak for itself."

So on that grand note the transaction was formalized, and following a small exchange of currency, accompanied by many exchanged courtesies, Mrs. Meade departed in possession of a bottle of Pollard's Proven Remedial Tonic, and an additional piece of information of which Mr. Hollister was entirely unaware.

* * *

The blinds in the hotel parlor were mostly closed, so that the mid-morning sunlight they admitted in thin strips was not enough to dispel the shadows behind the stiff mahogany-and-horsehair furniture, but it illuminated the fine particles of dust floating in the air that are to be found in all closed-up rooms. The dim lighting, the rather stark-looking potted plants standing up in the corners and the dust together gave the parlor somewhat of a funereal air. The impression was completed by the presence of Miss Asher, who was sitting bolt upright on the sofa when Mrs. Meade entered the room. Dorene Leighton sat in a chair near her aunt. She wore pale gray, and the shadows beneath her eyes were nearly the same color. Her eyes rested numbly on the floor; she seemed to have dwindled even smaller, as if all the spirit and life had gone out of her already small form. Mrs. Meade looked at her for a moment, and then turned toward Miss Asher, who had not moved except to turn a sharp disapproving eye in the direction of the intruder.

"Good morning," said Mrs. Meade in a low pleasant voice that did not disturb the hush of the parlor. "Is Sheriff Royal here yet? I had hoped to speak to him."

"No, he is not," said Miss Asher, in a tone which said that the icebergs at the North Pole had no intention of melting anytime soon either.

Mrs. Meade did not reply. With a gentle, polite smile that held the faintest breath of cool breeze itself, she sat down opposite the two ladies to wait.

Fortunately the wait was not long. In a moment or two there came a little noise outside, and the door opened. Andrew Royal escorted Clyde Renfrew into the room, giving him a little shove and regarding him with a grim expression and mutter that were probably for Miss Asher's benefit. Clyde's dejection of the previous day had been replaced by a kind of determined resignation, whether assumed for the encounter or not. He ventured a glance at Dorene as he sat down. Dorene was very white, her eyes fixed on the carpet straight in front of her.

Owing to a small request Mrs. Meade had made of him the evening before, Sheriff Royal had had since then to prepare an explanation for this moment, and had rehearsed at least a dozen on the walk from his office to the hotel with his prisoner — whom Miss Asher had not expected to see — but all of them had unkindly deserted him. He tried to ignore the expression directed toward him by that lady, and nearly kicked over one of the potted plants.

The voice came before he had found a chair for himself. "Really, Sheriff, I do *not* see that this is in any way helpful."

Royal landed himself in one of the mahogany chairs, which gave forth something between a creak and a crack. He opened his mouth to speak, then shut it again as though he had thought better of it, and looked over at Mrs. Meade. Miss Asher followed the glance with indignation.

Mrs. Meade stirred slightly in her chair. "It was I who asked Sheriff Royal to bring Clyde here," she said. "I thought it would be better this way."

Miss Asher brought voice, posture and look to bear upon Mrs. Meade in a way that usually made people retreat in meek apology. "Mrs. Meade, I do not know that this is any business of yours."

"Perhaps it isn't," Mrs. Meade agreed mildly. "And yet I cannot help occasionally interfering in things that are not my business when I see an opportunity for someone to do good by interfering. For instance, when—as now—I think I may be able to prevent a great mistake."

Dorene lifted her eyes from the carpet for a brief instant, a strange fleeting look that might have been hope and apprehension combined. "What— mistake?" said Miss Asher coldly, as if humoring a lunatic.

"The mistake of letting this outrageous accusation against Clyde Renfrew go on any longer," said Mrs. Meade. She turned to Andrew Royal. "You will simply have to drop those charges, Andrew. For there was no assault, there was no insult, and strangely enough there was not even a case of drunkenness...It was all a very clever scheme designed to extort money, and it was splendidly acted out—up to a point."

"What are you talking about?" said Clyde, breaking silence for the first time. He leaned forward a little.

By some miracle Miss Asher did not speak, and Mrs. Meade did. "It all fit together very well—almost too well. I had very nearly given up on making any sense of it besides the explanation given. But there was one small incident I could not account for in any way — the three taps I had heard a short time before the disturbance. Now, while it could not be proved, I personally felt sure the sound had come from Dorene Leighton's room. But *why?* If Clyde's story was true, he was not responsible; so it must have been Dorene. But here again — why? It was certainly no summons for help; it was a light measured tapping, more like a signal. But a signal for whom? The most likely person would have been Dorene's aunt, Miss Asher, who had the room on the left of hers. But *Miss Asher was out that afternoon*, and Dorene knew it. So the taps had to have been on the opposite wall — a signal to her accomplice, Mr. Hollister."

"Accom — "

"Let me tell you what *really* happened," said Mrs. Meade, interrupting Miss Asher with such ease that Andrew Royal could not help exulting over it even at such a moment. "Clyde came up to Dorene's room quite unsuspectingly on receipt of her note. The subject on which she wanted his advice was quite plausible, and the conversation initially went just as he recalls it. She offered him a glass of sherry, which he accepted. He may even have had a second glass. What he did not know was that the sherry in the decanter had been *drugged*. I believe there are certain drugs, you know, used by surgeons as anesthetics, which produce unconsciousness and whose aftereffects actually resemble those of intoxication. Mr. Hollister might very well have a certain knowledge of that. Gradually the drug began to take effect — and Clyde cannot remember what happened after that point! This was part of the plan. Dorene had only to get him to sit down so he would not stumble or fall and make some kind of a noise too soon—and then wait. She waited until about an hour had elapsed, possibly continuing to speak aloud from time to time so anyone passing the door would think a conversation was still going on. When the hour was up, or when Clyde showed signs of beginning to recover consciousness, she rose and tapped on the wall to summon Mr. Hollister, who had also been waiting. He came out and slipped into her room without anyone seeing or hearing him, and together they set the scene. The rest of the sherry in the decanter had to be disposed of, to give the impression that Clyde had drunk it—Mr. Hollister probably transferred it to an empty flask he carried for the purpose in his overcoat pocket. It was a small circumstance no one noticed, by the way, that he was wearing a heavy overcoat although it was a warm day!

"Following that, all he had to do was bang open the door, jerk Clyde to his feet and begin shaking him, and giving a very convincing performance of having just caught a drunken man insulting a young lady! Everyone who came running to see and hear accepted it at once—between the evidence of the decanter and Clyde's appearance, no one even questioned for a moment whether he was actually intoxicated. Unable to remember what had happened while he was under the influence of the drug, he even believed it himself.

"Of course, all this was only a guess," said Mrs. Meade modestly, "but I had an idea where evidence might be found. In order to pour the sherry from the decanter into the flask quickly and without spilling it, Mr. Hollister might have used a funnel, which he would also have carried in his overcoat pocket. With this in mind, I managed to blunder into his room yesterday—" Mrs. Meade permitted herself a smile at the recollection " — and examined his overcoat myself. And I found what I had expected — that the lining of one pocket smelled faintly of sherry."

There was a few seconds' silence. Then Miss Asher pulled herself up and went into action.

"This is all utterly ridiculous," she declared. "Preposterous. Do you really mean to assert, Mrs. Meade, that even if my niece were capable of inventing such a scheme to extort money and involving herself with that *odious* man Hollister, that she would be able to carry it out without my knowledge and without even—"

"I don't mean to assert that at all," said Mrs. Meade quite pleasantly. "You were a party to it yourself, Miss Asher."

A sudden sound came from Andrew Royal. It would not be an exaggeration to say that one of his wildest dreams had just come true.

"*I!* I declare, I have never been so—"

"I did briefly consider the theory that it could have been Dorene's own scheme — that she had wanted money to escape an overbearing guardian. But I dismissed that thought almost at once. She could have simply asked Clyde for a loan, if she trusted him; and it seemed unlikely that she would apply to Mr. Hollister for help. But once I considered you, Miss Asher, as a possible accomplice, the whole thing became beautifully clear at once. It was a necessary part of the plan for Dorene to have a punctilious relative to insist on reparation being made — if a shamed, shrinking girl were to so promptly insist herself on damages being paid, it might look strange.

"It was a complete scheme from the very

foundation, each person playing their part well. Mr. Hollister in his character as a salesman had the opportunity to mix with all sorts of people and find out about the character of any young man Miss Asher and her niece came into contact with, so they might choose a suitable victim for extortion. Clyde suited their purpose admirably—he was well-off financially; he was not accustomed to strong drink, and somewhat shy of women, which would make him easy to manipulate. Not even a good character would be able to overcome the appearances they crafted against him, with him unable...and perhaps unwilling...to defend himself."

Clyde turned his head, slowly, to look at Dorene. Her head was still down. Mrs. Meade looked at her too, and for a long moment there was silence. They were waiting. The silence seemed to build up against her, and she seemed to be resisting it without word or movement, but at last she could hold out no longer. Her face twisted with grief, a tremor ran all through her and she burst into tears. Deep sobs shook her as she leaned against the arm of the chair, covering her face with her hands. Clyde was still staring at her, as if he was still trying to understand.

"It's true," Dorene choked through her tears, "it's true, all of it. Mr. Hollister is my uncle—he and my aunt—his sister—it's the way they make our living—tricking people out of their money. They have all different ways. I've been with them since I was a little girl—I had nobody else, nowhere to go...and I was scared of being alone. They used to threaten to put me in an orphanage if I didn't keep quiet about what they did." She broke off for a second, another sob catching at her voice. "My uncle came up with this— this new scheme. He said I was old enough to help now and it was time I earned my keep. I didn't want to do it; I pleaded with him—but they threatened me, and—and I've always been a coward."

She drew out a handkerchief and futilely tried to blot the streaming tears from her face, with trembling hands. "I still tried to do something to spoil it—it was part of the plan that I wasn't supposed to want the money, but I really did try to tell the sheriff not to do anything—I tried, but my aunt—"

Her words died away in confusion and she subsided into muffled weeping, her head turned away against the back of the chair. Still no one else spoke; Clyde seemed in a daze, watching her.

Then Andrew Royal moved in his chair and found his voice. "I'll drop the charges, all right," he said. He got up. "And I'll bring a few more to replace 'em. Trying to squeeze money out of somebody on false pretenses is against the law too, you know, Miss Asher ma'am, and there'll be some answering done for that!"

Clyde came to life suddenly.

"Oh, no you don't," he said, rising and swinging to face the sheriff. "You're not going to charge anybody with anything, you hear? Because if you make out a case with one word in it involving Miss Leighton, I'll contradict everything."

He turned to Miss Asher, who had not made a sound or movement for the past several minutes, but was sitting rigidly, as if she feared moving even a muscle would bring about some calamity. "And you, you'd best clear out of here right now and not even think about coming back. This is one racket you're through with, anyway." He took one stride to the door and opened it. "Get out."

Miss Asher got out. She rose, very stiffly, and walked straight and mechanically through the door without looking right or left. Clyde shut it behind her with only a fraction less force than a bang.

Mrs. Meade rose to her feet.

"Where're *you* going?" barked Andrew Royal.

"Out," said Mrs. Meade. "You may as well come too, Andrew — I think our usefulness here is at an end."

As they passed through the doorway Mrs. Meade looked back. Dorene was still weeping, her wet crumpled handkerchief pressed to her face. As Mrs. Meade looked, Clyde got down on his knees beside the chair, looking rather helpless, but also as though he very much wanted to say something. He moved his hand, and hesitantly touched Dorene's arm. Then the door closed.

Andrew Royal was still fuming. He did not speak until they had got nearly to the end of the hallway, and then he blew out a puff of breath in a snort that seemed to dissipate some of his pent-up irritation. "Well, there's another one gone and made a prize fool of himself," he said.

"Perhaps," said Mrs. Meade, "but dear me, Andrew, that poor little creature needs someone to take care of her — and Clyde is just the one to do it."

"All this'll make a nice thing for him to cast up to her if he's ever got a mind to," said Royal.

"I don't think he will. With some people, you know, compassion is always stronger than any sense of injury. I think Clyde will always see Dorene as the trapped, frightened girl who needed rescuing from her own worse troubles. He's finally found someone who *needs* the love and protection he can give her."

"H'm," said Royal, grudgingly.

"She was wrong, of course, very wrong—but she has suffered a great deal for it already, I think. Think of what it must have been like for her, sitting up there in that room for an hour, watching and waiting for Clyde to recover consciousness, knowing all that time that it was through *her* that he was to be made a victim of their scheme—especially with the way she felt about him."

"What way she felt about him?" demanded Royal.

"Why, she was in love with him, of course. Anyone could see that."

"They could, eh?" said Andrew Royal.

They came into the hotel lobby, where the clerk was standing behind the desk looking toward the front door with a mildly surprised expression, pen in hand. "Is Miss Asher in?" Mrs. Meade inquired of him.

"Why, no, ma'am," said the clerk. "She just checked out and left, in rather a hurry—and Mr. Hollister, the commercial traveling man, he went with her. She said she'd send for her luggage!"

* * *

"Incredible," declared Miss Powers warmly, "quite incredible!"

"I never did like the woman," said Miss Brewster robustly. "Thought a good deal too much of herself. The airs she put on! Well, all the people she snubbed in Sour Springs can at least take comfort that it was all an act."

"It may have been all an act, to be sure," said Mrs. Clairborn, smiling, "but I have a feeling Miss

Asher enjoyed it."

Phyllis Clairborn leaned over and whispered to Mrs. Meade under cover of the animated conversation going on around them. "However *did* you know?" she said. "None of us would ever have spotted Miss Asher as a confidence trickster, not in a million years!"

"Well, you and your mother helped, as a matter of fact," said Mrs. Meade, unable to entirely conceal a little half-embarrassed smile at the flattery. "Your mother remarked upon the fact that there was something a little unnatural in the way Miss Asher conducted the whole affair. Sheriff Royal commented on it, too, without realizing its significance. Rather than trying to hush up a scandal, she practically made a show out of her indignation, and made sure everyone knew about it. People *do* enjoy talking about scandal, I'm afraid, but only when it doesn't concern them or someone they love — *or have responsibility for*. In a genuine situation Miss Asher ought to have said very little, and only obtained Miss Powers' sympathy with a few plaintive sighs and looks." Phyllis choked back a giggle, the description of the two ladies' interaction was so perfectly accurate. "But instead she and Mr. Hollister both played their parts so as to attract plenty of attention — why, he nearly turned the hotel upside-down with his performance! There was even the detail of the room number being omitted from Dorene's note to Clyde — so he had to inquire at the desk and draw attention to his presence there. I think," said Mrs. Meade meditatively, "it was that feeling of unreality which first gave me the notion that there was something wrong somewhere. It was in the back of my mind all the time. Later when I was thinking very hard trying to make sense of the taps on the wall, all the pieces fell into place."

"And how did *I* help?" queried Phyllis.

"Well, you called my attention to another small but curious thing—that Dorene had seemed unhappy in love, even though there was every indication that the feeling between her and Clyde was mutual. She knew and dreaded, you see, what was going to happen to him."

"If it had only been a play, some of it would have been awfully funny," said Phyllis. "The way Miss Asher and Mr. Hollister went on, him swaggering around being as loud and uncivilized as he could, and Miss Asher putting her nose in the air when she went past and pretending to detest him! But I don't suppose Dorene thought it was very funny," she added, with the quick change to perceptiveness that was so characteristic of her.

"No," agreed Mrs. Meade, "there are many things that look quite different depending on which side of them you look from. The important thing, I think, is being able to look *back* on things in such a way that they don't hurt you too badly."

"Do you think Dorene will be able to?" said Phyllis, with an intent, quizzical glance.

"Yes," said Mrs. Meade, "I think she will."

THE
OLDEST FLAME

*A man would incur any danger for a woman…would
even die for her! But if this were done simply
with the object of winning her, where was that real love of
which sacrifice of self on behalf of another is the truest proof?*

~ Anthony Trollope

Mrs. Meade gazed with much pleasure and contentment over the view from the garden bench where she sat. Below the well-kept gardens of the other houses strung out down the slope of the hill, a silvery glimpse of the river in the valley twinkled bright in the afternoon sun, with a lovely vista of wooded hills rising beyond it. Here in the garden, the air of the summer afternoon was soft and peaceful, with bees humming among the flowers and now and then the sweet piercing song of a bird from the trees high overhead.

Mrs. Meade looked around the garden again, her admiration mixed with something like marveling. The latter expression was accompanied by a touch of motherly fondness as she turned to look at her companion, who was leaning against the tree which cast its shade over the bench.

"How you have grown, Mark!" she said. "The last time I saw you, you were just a rambunctious schoolboy. And now look at the fine young college man you've grown into."

Mark Lansbury grinned with just a touch of self-consciousness. He was a dark, good-looking boy of nineteen, tall and athletic, with a pair of arresting, expressive brown eyes. With Mrs. Meade, whom he had always regarded in the light of a favorite aunt, he was always at his ease, and did not find it necessary to observe the dignity that had become rather more important to him since attaining the aforementioned collegiate status.

"Everything seems to have moved very quickly for your family these past few years," said Mrs. Meade. "Your father's promotion—this beautiful new house— and then you off to college. I've missed seeing all of you, these years you've been so busy. I was so very happy when I received your mother's invitation last month, to find she had remembered me."

"She could never forget you!" said Mark warmly. "None of us could. Mother was always thinking about you, even when things were busiest. I've heard her speak of you a hundred times."

"Well, as things have turned out, I'm glad she chose this summer to invite me, since the Greys are here. It's been so good to see them again too."

Mark did not answer this. He picked at the smooth bark of the tree, looking down at the grass at Mrs. Meade's feet, the animation of a moment before gone from his face. Mrs. Meade observed him quietly for a moment, and then, in a voice and manner so light.

and natural it could never have aroused any suspicion of ulterior motives, entered on an entirely new subject

"How do you like college?" she said. "Your father told me you were doing very well, but you've hardly said a word about it since I've been here. Was your first year a good one?"

"Oh, yes, it was fine," said Mark, shying a broken bit of bark at the ground. "But to tell you the truth, I haven't been thinking much about college lately."

"There's something else on your mind, then?" said Mrs. Meade, who had already divined as much.

"Some*one* else, anyway," Mark mumbled, looking down again with a little color in his face.

"My dear boy, don't tell me you've tumbled into a love-affair already!"

"Oh, I didn't tumble," said Mark, looking over at her with an uneasy smile, as if he already half regretted sharing his secret. "It's been coming on steadily enough." He paused. "It's Rose, of course. Could you even think it was anyone else?"

There was something different in his voice as he spoke these last words, a subtle ring of feeling that made Mrs. Meade look up at him with closer attention. His restless eyes met hers for an instant. Yes, he had grown up a good deal, she thought. Sensitive, earnest, impatient, ardent—all those qualities of youth were there in abundance, but somewhere along the way a door had opened to the capacity for a deeper feeling, one likely to throw all those very qualities into turmoil.

"Rose," she said thoughtfully. Mark nodded, watching her as if hoping to gain some sort of encouragement from her response.

"I knew you were always good friends when

you were children, but I didn't know you felt that way about her."

"Well, I do now," said Mark. "I'm in love with her — miserably in love with her, Mrs. Meade, but she doesn't care whether I'm alive or dead."

Mrs. Meade forbid herself to smile. She had long since learned to balance her sense of humor with her expression of sympathy, and Mark Lansbury was intensely in earnest.

"That seems rather unlikely," she said. "Does Rose know yet how you feel?"

"She knows I'm in love with her. I've told her so. But she doesn't take me seriously. She thinks it's just an infatuation and I'll get over it." He swung round so his back was against the trunk of the tree. "I used to think, at first, that maybe…"

A wistful look came over his face for a few seconds, but then it vanished and his mouth set bitterly. He thrust his hands deep in his pockets. "But she's never been the same since she met that Steven Emery. She'd believe anything he told her, whether it was the truth or not."

Mrs. Meade had been introduced to Steven Emery for the first time the evening before, and she understood the complication to Mark's problem.

"Who is Mr. Emery exactly? I thought at first that he was a friend of your father's."

"No. The Greys met him somehow in Denver last winter, and he's been hanging around them ever since. Mr. Grey introduced him to Dad when Dad was in the city on business. That's why he got included in the invitation when Mother asked the Greys down here, I think. Dad's trying to get him to invest in the new railroad project he wants to put through, because

Emery's supposed to have money. But I don't think he's biting. He's too busy entertaining Rose."

"Is that why he came down here, do you think?" said Mrs. Meade.

Mark gave a disheartened shrug. "I don't know whether he has any serious intentions, or if he's just amusing himself. He's a lot older than her, you know. But I *am* serious. How can I make Rose see that?"

"Have you tried poetry?" suggested the practical Mrs. Meade.

"I wrote a lot," said Mark, "and then tore it up. Rose would only laugh at it. But if it was Steven Emery or someone else like him writing her sonnets, she'd think it grand. It's all a matter of perception — the way she sees me," he added, as if he felt it necessary to explain for Mrs. Meade's benefit.

Mrs. Meade did not entirely succeed in hiding her smile this time, since she had spent a good portion of this conversation trying to adjust her own perception of the parties in question. The image that still came most vividly to her mind was one she had seen from her window some years before, of an eight-year-old Rose and eleven-year-old Mark constructing a river and dam in the mud of a ditch below the railway embankment. But that was before prosperity, in the form of railroads, had descended upon both families — and girlhood upon Rose.

"Nothing I can say will make any difference to Rose," Mark was saying. "My trouble is that there's nothing I can *do*. I've got no way of showing her what I'm made of."

"No, there are few dragons to slay in our everyday life," said Mrs. Meade thoughtfully. "But do you know, I've always thought the girls who would take a man on his dragon-slaying merits rather short-sighted. There are plenty of men who can rise to the occasion when something extraordinary happens, but what about the little things — the common things? Those are what will matter most in the rest of their life together."

"I don't know," said Mark. "I've always thought the crisis shows the essence of a man's character — the trial by fire, so to speak. How he answers to that gives you the clue to everything else about him."

"How do you think you would be in a crisis?" inquired Mrs. Meade, gravely, but with a genial twinkle in her eye.

Mark reddened a little, but he answered, "I'd *like* to think I'd come out well...but I don't see how I'll ever have the opportunity."

"Don't give up, Mark," said Mrs. Meade, putting her hand out to him with a warm, affectionate manner that acted upon him so far as to bring a somewhat forlorn smile to his face. "Rose is young yet — she may not know just what it is she wants. But don't waste all your time waiting for your grand chance. Just be 'faithful in that which is least' — and perhaps one day you'll find your chance is come."

"Do you really think I could make my own chance...that way?" said Mark, sounding a little doubtful, but with a somewhat vacant look in his eyes, as if he was turning over an idea in his mind.

"Perhaps you could. Who knows?" said Mrs. Meade, smiling again.

"Yes," said Mark, "who knows."

* * *

When Mrs. Meade came through the open French window into the sunny lower hall, a woman was just coming down the staircase opposite. She was dressed for the evening, in white with a pale peach-colored sash, a very simply cut dress that suited her tall, spare style of beauty in such a way that Mrs. Meade inadvertently paused to admire the effect. She had been introduced to Eloisa Parrish on the preceding evening and had been similarly struck by her appearance, but had had little or no success in forming an acquaintance with her. Miss Parrish was a handsome young woman of twenty-seven or twenty-eight, with a certain austerity about her finely molded features and an almost haughty lift to her narrow chin. She had remained silent and aloof through most of the evening in the drawing-room, seemingly unmoved by any kind of pleasantry or any topic of conversation.

She paused for half an instant on the lowest stair as her eyes fell on Mrs. Meade, as if she had not expected to encounter anyone here or did not particularly want to. Mrs. Meade, however, did not see this movement, or perhaps chose not to see it.

"Oh, good afternoon, Miss Parrish," she said pleasantly. "I was just on my way up to dress for dinner. It has been so fine out that I've spent most of the day outdoors. Have you seen much of the garden?"

"No," said Miss Parrish with the barest of polite smiles, a slight curve of the lips that did not mean much. "No, I have hardly been out of my room today."

"I hope you are not feeling ill?" said Mrs. Meade. Her direct, yet considerate eyes took stock of the younger woman's face. "You look a little pale, if I may say so."

A door opened somewhere in the direction of

the drawing-room and voices drifted out, and over them rose the sound of a young girl's happy laugh. Neither woman's eyes wavered, but an almost contemptuous expression passed across Miss Parrish's face.

She lifted her chin slightly, though not, Mrs. Meade thought, so much with defiance as with the air of one who would conceal some emotion. "I must have had a headache, I suppose," said Miss Parrish in a cool, ironical voice. "At least that is what I must say if I'm asked. That is what we all say, isn't it, to hide a more embarrassing ailment — the desire for solitude."

Without another word she moved past Mrs. Meade and went out through the French window onto the terrace. Mrs. Meade looked after her with a slightly perplexed expression, but at nearly the same moment she heard footsteps behind her and turned back as Mrs. Lansbury came into the hall.

Mrs. Lansbury had entered in time to see Miss Parrish disappear through the window, and to observe the expression on Mrs. Meade's face, and there was understanding in the smile which she exchanged with her friend.

"I hope I haven't done anything to offend her," said Mrs. Meade.

"Oh, no," said Mrs. Lansbury. "It isn't you. That's just the way she is — now." She looked out of the window, and then the two women began slowly to ascend the stairs together. "I invited her here in hopes of improving her spirits a bit, but so far it doesn't seem to have succeeded. She's just come back from California, you see, after spending some years out there. I hadn't heard from her in quite a long time until recently. She doesn't tell me much, but I gather that there was a—an unhappy love-affair of some sort out there, which seems to have left her rather bitter."

"Dear me, not another one," murmured Mrs. Meade.

"You know all of our little dramas already, I see," said Mrs. Lansbury with a smile.

"*Little* dramas?"

"Well—they seem that way, against the backdrop of a big world. But I know they are terribly big and important to the young people living them." They paused for a moment on the first-floor landing. "That's why it's pleasant to grow older, in a way—you gain the ability to take things a little more levelly. But it is rather distressing not to be able to feel the sympathy for those passionate young ones that you ought, just because you feel that *you* could handle their troubles more easily if you were in their place." She smiled affectionately at Mrs. Meade. "But you, I think, have never lost the ability to see things through everyone's eyes. That's the thing that is special about you."

"Oh, dear, no—not special," said Mrs. Meade. "It's really only taking an interest in things—or rather, in people. One must have some kind of an interest in life, after all," she said, quietly, "and I can't think of one more rewarding."

"If a little trying, at times," said Mrs. Lansbury.

"You mustn't ever think I mind being made a confidant, if that's what you are suggesting," said Mrs. Meade.

Mrs. Lansbury laughed. "Very well! You may consider yourself established as the official confidant of our party. I just hope"—and her smile may have been slightly shadowed with unease—"that we won't have too much need of you."

* * *

It was curious, thought Mrs. Meade, that the party gathered around the dinner table should be composed of so many individual cases of despondency and failure. Taken in theory, the people collected here ought to have made very good company. But there was something amiss with each which kept them from being their usual selves, and cast a decided damper over the proceedings. There was Miss Parrish wrapped in the silence of her own wrongs, Mark and his unhappy love. And there seemed to be something brewing in the business sector as well. Both Mr. Lansbury and Mr. Grey bore the abstracted look that seemed to indicate they were thinking of something that dinner had called them away from, and that they were looking ahead to the moment when they could take it up again. In the intervals when the main flow of conversation passed them by, they talked in low voices across the corner of the table. And Mrs. Lansbury, as the hostess, could hardly fail to sense the effect these undercurrents were having on the general tenor of the party she had put together. The only two people who seemed entirely happy and at their ease — aside from Mrs. Grey, whom Mrs. Meade mentally counted aside as the light-hearted, unperceptive sort of woman who seldom notices things which lie beneath the surface — were Rose Grey and Steven Emery.

Rose was alive with youth and spirits, glowing like a little rose with happiness at simply being where she was, at the pleasure of entertaining and being entertained, and at the attention that her dinner companion devoted to her. That this meant much to her was evident in the quick, eager little sideways glances she turned up to Steven Emery as he talked, and the shy, pleased smile that quivered on her lips when he gave his attention to something she said. Their conversation ran on easily, often including Mrs. Grey, regardless of the silence or hesitancy of the others at the table.

Rose was a child still, Mrs. Meade thought as she watched her, but she was at the age where young girls wish to be as grown-up as possible and scorn youthful things — hence her attraction to the older, distinguished Steven Emery and her tendency to look down on her old childhood playmate. It was unfortunate, too, that Mark, on the other side of the table, was incapable of concealing just how hard he was taking it. For most of the meal his eyes had been on Rose, the hurt in them plain at every word she exchanged with her companion. Beside Steven Emery, who had the good grace not to notice his hostility, he appeared merely a jealous and somewhat sullen boy.

And yet even Steven Emery seemed to have something on his mind. Occasionally when Rose was talking animatedly to her mother or someone else, Mrs. Meade observed him stealing a look at her that seemed considering, possibly a little doubtful. Was he wondering if he would be able to win her? All the signs certainly looked favorable. He was said to be well-off financially; he seemed an acceptable suitor in every personal respect. Perhaps he was merely attacked with the self-doubt that sometimes overtakes a man in love. He did not look like a man who lost his self-possession often. In his early thirties, yet hand-some enough to look younger, well-dressed and with a distinct charm of manner, he certainly had every advantage calculated to make a good impression. Mrs. Meade, fond as she was of Mark Lansbury, had to acknowledge that there was no good reason why Rose should *not* fall in love with Steven Emery.

"It's only the time that makes it difficult," Mr. Lansbury was saying, turning a small silver fork over slowly in his fingers. "If I had an immediate prospect of capital to show him it would be a different matter altogether."

"I wouldn't be upset if you fail this once — you've had so many successes. Everything *you* do seems to go right," Grey added, with a slight laugh that did not quite succeed.

"Well, you may have something there," said Lansbury. "Perhaps I am too used to having things go my way. Unfortunate for me, if so, but I'm afraid it doesn't affect my belief in this project."

"You can't fault Thornton for doing things in order," observed Grey.

"No," said Lansbury dryly, "except when it inconveniences me."

There was a general laugh at this, a slight lull in the conversation having made these remarks audible to the rest of the table. The two gentlemen looked up, smiling a little, though it was clear they knew there was less humor in the remark than any of the others appreciated. Mrs. Lansbury may have known, for she sent her husband a gently appealing look from the foot of the table which seemed to ask that he leave business topics for another time. He answered with a look of comprehension and a barely perceptible nod.

"Always railroads!" said Rose to Steven Emery in an undertone, with a pretty little look and smile that was also meant to be one of understanding. He had been listening abstractedly to the other men for a moment, a shade of thoughtfulness on his face, and she guessed that the subject did not interest him.

Whatever the case, he returned the smile. "I shouldn't despise them, if I were you. Among other things, they may be the reason we are all sitting here at this table tonight."

"What do you mean?" said Rose.

"Well, aren't they directly responsible for your father's and Mr. Lansbury's success? If one wants to be quite literal about it, we can attribute the very roof over our heads and the salad on our plates to the first pickaxe-blows struck on Carver Cut."

"Oh, of course," said Rose, smiling. "And I don't despise them by any means! I was nearly as interested in the construction as Papa was last winter, and I enjoyed it when he took me to see the work at the Cut. But I'm afraid I've never been able to take an interest in the part of railroad business that concerns stocks and shares and such, so I should be left in the dust if the talk turned that way."

"Well," said Steven Emery, smiling, in a slightly lower voice, "you could be no less lovely listening than speaking."

It was low enough that Mrs. Meade only caught a part of the words, but Mark and Miss Parrish both heard it. The effect on the former may be imagined, and it did nothing to improve the latter's humor either. All evening Miss Parrish had been regarding Rose's merriment with an air of disapproval worthy of an unfeeling spinster aunt. The line of her fine, almost colorless lips expressed something that approached dislike every time she looked across at the younger girl. Every manifestation of light-heartedness on Rose's part seemed to grate on her, and she did not even make an attempt to hide it.

Rose could not speak for a full moment. The conflicting feelings of delight and shyness glowed on her face like changing lights, and she did something with her napkin on the edge of the table to hide her confusion, looking for the moment even younger than she was. Steven Emery seemed a little amused as well as gratified at the effect of his compliment — and he had the delicacy to wait until Rose's heartbeat had steadied before he spoke again.

He leaned toward her slightly. "Perhaps this is not the best conversation for a dinner-table either."

Rose flashed him a quick, daring glance from her bright, long-lashed gray eyes. "Then you will have to think of another place!"

* * *

After dinner the ladies withdrew to the library, a large, pleasant room at the rear of the house that overlooked the garden through several long French windows, which stood partly open to admit the cool evening breeze. Mrs. Lansbury and Mrs. Grey sat down together by common accord, but Miss Parrish took a seat at some distance from them — and Mrs. Meade, after a few seconds' consideration, crossed the room and sat down in a chair rather near to Miss Parrish than otherwise. She would have been assured of a pleasant time in the company of her friends, but somehow she did not feel it right to leave Miss Parrish alone. Miss Parrish might choose to draw apart, might not wish to be disturbed, but at least she should not have the opportunity to indulge in self-pity over the fact that no one wanted to be near her — a reaction Mrs.

Meade judged as likely to follow as any other.

Rose did not sit, but wandered lightly about the room, looking at the titles of the books on the shelves and at the oil painting above the fireplace, and eventually came to stand at one of the windows, a few yards away from where Miss Parrish and Mrs. Meade sat in pensive but not unfriendly silence. Mrs. Meade's eyes rested on Rose with a touch of the same fondness they had earlier shown towards Mark. She had known Rose as a little child, and now she was seeing her growing up into a woman. She was so unconsciously lovely as she stood there with the tint of the sunset light falling over her, one slender hand resting on the edge of the open window, with her rich deep-gold curls swept up in that new grown-up style that was still curious to see framing the familiar little features of her face. And Mrs. Meade became aware that Miss Parrish was silently watching the girl too, from her chair in the shadow, and wondered why the gulf between those two, separated only by moderate differences in age, character and style of beauty, should in this instance be so very large.

It was while she was thinking this that she saw Rose's expression change, and her attitude become one of definite consciousness. Mrs. Meade looked out through the window into the garden and saw that Steven Emery had just come into view there, walking slowly with his hands in his pockets. He glanced up toward the window, and smiled as he saw Rose standing there. The smile was an invitation. Rose gave a quick glance over her shoulder toward her mother, then slipped out through the open window and went toward the edge of the terrace.

Mrs. Meade looked over at Miss Parrish, whose

face had settled once more into that set look of dis-approval. Perhaps her glance asked a question, but at any rate Miss Parrish felt called upon to speak.

"It is difficult for me to understand why a self-centered child should be such an attractive thing to so many people," she said.

"Rose may be a little flighty," admitted Mrs. Meade. "But I do believe she has good sense at heart. Most young girls go through a time when they particularly relish what may seem like frivolity to us."

There was a slight emphasis on the "us" that would have made most women flinch a little under the gentle irony, for a greater difference than the one between the elegant younger woman and mild, middle-aged Mrs. Meade could hardly be found. But Miss Parrish did not seem to notice.

"That is something which experience will cure her of soon enough," she said, looking out of the window.

She said nothing more, and so they sat silently again for a few moments until the sound of footsteps and voices in the hall betokened the approach of the men.

It was Mark who opened the door and came into the room a few steps in advance of the others, his eyes already going from one person to another in search of the one. It took him only seconds to see that Rose was not there. His eyes fell upon the open window. A look of comprehension and resentment overspread his face, and he turned abruptly away into a corner of the room.

Mr. Lansbury had entered closely followed by Mr. Grey, but their bearing and brisk pace indicated they had come for some specific purpose rather than to join the party. Lansbury went directly over to his wife and took her hand. "My dear, I hope you won't mind if we abandon you for a day or two," he said. "I've just had a telegram from Thornton in Denver, and I've decided I ought to go there and see him about it. George is going to accompany me."

"It's nothing serious, I hope?" said Mrs. Lansbury, looking up at him with subtle questioning in her eyes that seemed to ask more than she would say before all the room.

Lansbury shook his head. Mrs. Meade thought he looked rather tired and harried, as though whatever business he had in hand at the moment was weighing on him more than he liked. "No. I just feel I can be more persuasive about this investment business in person than I can by telegraph. There's no sense in letting him turn me down just because I didn't make an opportunity to speak to him."

"I see. How long will you be gone?"

"Not more than a few days, if all goes well. We could possibly be back by the day after tomorrow."

Mark, in the corner, was leaning against the bookcase with a restive air, casting uneasy glances toward the French window as if he was trying to make up his mind to do something. Mrs. Meade knew it was only a matter of time before he followed Rose. With this thought, she stood up. It would be regrettable for the already uncomfortable evening to end with some sort of scene, which was a distinct possibility if Mark were to go out by himself and join the two in the garden while in this mood. So Mrs. Meade essayed a spiking of guns.

"Will you walk outside with me, Mark?" she said. "I would very much like to go round the garden again, and see it in the evening."

A bit reluctantly, she thought, but evidently knowing there was no way to refuse without her knowing why, Mark came forward and opened the window the rest of the way for Mrs. Meade to pass through. They went out and down the few shallow steps from the terrace, and Mrs. Meade took Mark's arm as they turned to walk along the level lawn to the right. It was an unspoken agreement that they should go that way.

It was a beautiful evening. The setting sun cast streams of gold light over the smooth green lawn and lit up the flowers that stood against its rays like translucent jewels. Away to the left, the valley was falling into shadows of muted color with occasional spangles of light on the tops of the trees, and the clouds above it on the western skyline were a white and gold glory almost too bright to look at. Mrs. Meade, knowing full well that nothing she said was of any consequence, talked on gently about the loveliness of the flowers and about the sunset, while Mark, his eyes searching ahead, murmured an occasional indistinct word of agreement without even hearing what it was he was answering.

At last they rounded a clump of shrubs that brought them in sight of the curving stone wall that bounded this end of the garden. The wall was higher than a man's head, but served only an ornamental purpose, for it joined to nothing on either end. It was overgrown with a tangle of climbing roses that had crept down and overtaken the flowerbeds at its base and thrown flower-hung grapples across into the trees that stood near it, a fairylike tapestry draped on the rough-hewn stone. The sun struck over the wall and made the corner a pool of light, and Rose Grey and Steven Emery were standing here facing one another, a little apart, with Rose the nearest to the wall. As Mrs. Meade and Mark came into view of them Steven Emery spoke, and his voice carried clearly to their ears. "This is the perfect background for you, Rose," he said. He was leaning back slightly as if to take in to its fullest effect the picture that she made. "It must have been something more than chance that went into giving you your name, because these flowers are your very own."

Rose at this instant became aware of the observers, and her face flooded with color. She turned with slightly overdone carelessness toward the wall, and touched the petals of a half-blown pink rose with her fingertips as if the flowers, and not her companion, were her primary interest at the moment. "Oh, no," she said. "I'm just the shadow — these are the real thing. You could never find anything lovelier than — that, for instance." She pointed to a deep crimson rose, opened to full velvety perfection, which hung just on the edge of the wall above their heads.

She looked over her shoulder at Steven Emery, and smiled a little. "The best ones are always out of reach, aren't they."

"Nothing is ever completely out of reach," said Steven Emery gallantly, and stepping into the flowerbed, he found a foothold on the projecting edge of a stone, reached up to grasp one of the sturdiest vines and pulled himself up to where he could stretch out his hand and pluck the crimson rose. Mrs. Meade, who had released Mark's arm, came to stand beside Rose as they watched Emery twist the flower from the vine and then descend. He stepped out of the bed, and held the flower out to Rose. It was very simply done, and yet the moment somehow seemed to have a great weight.

"Thank you," said Rose. She was looking down at the flower, and spoke in a level, somewhat constrained voice—perhaps because she knew that Mark, standing a few feet apart with his hands in his pockets, was watching her, and knew what sort of expression was on his face. "You didn't have to do that, Mr. Emery."

"It's nothing," said Steven Emery quietly. "Any man would be willing to do—a great deal more for you, Miss Grey, and not call it a hardship."

And Mrs. Meade, observing the look in his eyes as he spoke, judged from it that whatever else he might be thinking, he was at least serious in his intentions toward Rose.

* * *

Mrs. Meade had not found time to unpack her satchel after her arrival the evening before. On this night, as she was preparing for bed, she gave the bag a speculative look, and then decided it could just as well be left till morning. She sighed as she concluded this. She felt unaccountably tired. The day had contained no real physical exertion, but mental strain can make one more unpleasantly tired than a simple hard day's work, and the consciousness that things are not right with the people around us thus affects a perceptive mind.

Mrs. Meade was thinking again of others' problems as she brushed out her thick graying hair before the bureau mirror, in her dressing-gown, by the light of a single candle. Had it been only a dinner-party, she thought, things would have been different — certain tensions might have been diffused at least for the time being by the parting of the people whose presence affected each other. But the Lansburys' guests were due to stay here in the same house for at least a week. Mrs. Meade sighed again. She thought of the look of frustrated misery Mark had worn all evening. It must be hard to see a rival successfully winning away the object of your affections under your own roof. She only hoped it would not result in further unhappiness before the week was out.

She finished braiding her hair, and blew out the candle. The night was still warm, so her window was open a few inches. Mrs. Meade raised the sash further and pushed back the curtains to admit the breeze, and then went to bed.

She woke suddenly several hours later. The room was darker, but the house was not silent — she was conscious at once of a commotion below. The vibration of a slamming door, running footsteps and a man's voice shouting. It took her a few seconds to comprehend the words, and then the sense of them came all at once as she recognized the strong smell of smoke: "Fire! fire! Get up — the house is on fire!"

Hastily Mrs. Meade climbed out of bed and reached for her dressing-gown. With one arm into the sleeve she bent over to put on her slippers. As she straightened up, her eyes fell on the open window, with her satchel sitting on a chair just beneath it. It was the work of an instant to seize the bag and throw it through the window, and in another instant she had opened her bedroom door and was outside in the hall, tying the sash of her dressing-gown as she went. The hall was smoky, and an uneven flaring light was coming up from the staircase, accompanied by the muffled sound of women's shrieks. Mrs. Meade turned the other way. Miss Parrish's room was just round the corner of the hall from hers, and the door was shut. Mrs. Meade beat on the door and called out, "Miss Parrish! Miss Parrish, wake up! — fire!"

There was no response. Mrs. Meade tried the door, but it was locked. "Miss Parrish!" she called again. She glanced about her. The smoke was growing thicker; it was dangerous to stay even a moment longer. Mrs. Meade turned and hurried back down the hall, coughing, her hand over her mouth. She descended the stairs to the first-floor landing. Over the banister she caught a glimpse of Mrs. Grey and Rose, her long, loose golden plait of hair streaming over her shoulder, hurrying down the next set of stairs to the ground floor.

As she reached the landing, where the smoke was not so bad, Mark Lansbury came running out of the opposite corridor, disheveled and wide-eyed with alarm, and nearly collided with her. "Where's Rose?" he cried.

Instead of answering Mrs. Meade seized his arm and pointed back up the stairs she had come down. "Miss Parrish is locked in her room and doesn't answer! You'll have to try and break in the door — hurry!"

"All right — I'll — " For an instant Mark seemed to hesitate, cast one distraught glance around and then bolted up the stairs. Mrs. Meade hurried on downward. The lower hall was filled with smoke, and the doorways of the various rooms were blazing. The front door was open, and a cluster of women clad in nightgowns and shawls and dressing-gowns were milling on the lawn just outside—the cook, two maids, Mrs. Grey and her daughter. Mrs. Lansbury was there, white-faced but composed, and at the edge of the agitated group was the tall, reassuring figure of Steven Emery, his resolute voice rising above the clamor and restoring some measure of order. "Nobody's hurt? Good—is everyone here?"

Mrs. Meade pushed her way through the group with some difficulty until she was near enough to Emery to make herself heard. "Mr. Emery—Mr. Emery, Mark is still inside, and Miss Parrish. She was shut in her room, and I sent him up to help her."

Emery sent a swift glance through the doorway of the burning house, up the staircase that was now glowing with fierce orange light. There was a crack and then a splintering sound from one of the downstairs rooms, and a tongue of flame flashed through its doorway and retreated. "I'd better help him. Keep them away—" He raised his voice. "All of you—get well away from the house, and stay away! The butler's gone for help." He put the women out of his way and ducked through the front door into the house, as another crash sounded from somewhere inside.

All the windows on the ground floor were bright with that terrible orange radiance as the group of women made their way across the lawn, picking their steps over the dew-wet grass in the wavering light the fire threw, and huddled together near the flower border on the far side. Mrs. Grey wilted to the ground sobbing hysterically, and beside her Mrs. Lansbury's little maid was shivering and crying more quietly, while Rose, strung up to a pitch of fear and excitement, distractedly tried to calm them both. Mrs. Meade, standing with one hand at her throat, was watching the unnatural light grow slowly in the upper windows, her lips moving in silent prayer for those still inside. The minutes seemed to stretch out endlessly, while the fire raged on without opposition. Would the whole house be consumed before anything could be done to stop it?

Then from down the hill came a faint shout, and Mrs. Meade looked back to see several bobbing points of light coming along the dark road, lanterns in the hands of neighbors responding to the butler's summons for help. Mrs. Lansbury left the group and hurried down the lawn to meet them.

In the same moment the cook and the other maid both uttered a dismayed cry. Mrs. Meade turned—a figure lurched from the smoking front door of the house, a man bent under a heavy burden. There was a rush of flames against the glass of the nearest window, and their bright light fell upon him. Rose screamed. It was Steven Emery, with Mark Lansbury over his shoulder.

Her heart in her throat, Mrs. Meade moved forward stiffly to meet him. When he had got within ten feet of the group on the lawn Emery swayed to a halt, overbalanced and went to one knee, tumbling the unconscious Mark into the grass. He got back to his feet as Mrs. Meade reached them and knelt beside Mark. She felt Rose's hand clutch tightly at her shoulder from behind.

"He isn't hurt," said Emery hoarsely. "The smoke overcame him. He'll be all right in a moment."

"But Miss Parrish!" cried Mrs. Meade.

"I'm going back after her." He turned and ran back toward the house.

Mrs. Meade loosened Mark's collar, noting,

with the ironic clarity with which inconsequent details stand out in moments of chaos, that his shirt had been misbuttoned, and moved his head to an easier position in the grass. Rose, after watching for a few seconds, cast an anguished look at the blazing house and then fled back to her mother, stumbling over the ruffled hem of her dressing-gown as she went. The men whom the butler had brought were at work now, bringing buckets of water from the pump by the stables in through the front door and rushing out with the empty ones in a swirl of smoke.

Out on the lawn, the only sounds beside the crackle of the flames and an occasional distant shout from one of the workers were Mrs. Grey's and the little maid's sobs, and Rose gasping and whispering as she knelt by her mother's side, one arm around her — whether prayers or comfort for her mother or both. Mrs. Meade fanned Mark steadily with the little maid's nightcap, the only thing handy, her attention divided between him and the upper corner of the house, from which foreboding wreaths of smoke were now ascending, ghostly grey against the black ceiling of the night. Steven Emery had not yet reappeared.

In a few moments Mark's eyelashes flickered, and he moved one arm slightly. He coughed, turning on one side with the convulsive motion, and then lay still for a moment, blinking dazedly up at the flaming spectacle that towered over them.

His eyes found Mrs. Meade's face bending solicitously above him, and he made a confused effort at speech. "Where — what did I —"

"You're all right, dear. You were overcome by the smoke — Mr. Emery had to carry you out."

"And Rose — and Mother —"

"They're safe."

Mark gave a bitter laugh, which turned into a strangled cough. He tipped his head back and shut his eyes. "My grand chance!" he said thickly. "It couldn't have been planned any better. And all I do is get made a fool of—again."

A loud crack from somewhere overhead made Mrs. Meade look up. There were shouts from over near the house and several men dashed out from the front door as if pursued—in the brief second her glance went in their direction Mrs. Meade thought she recognized Steven Emery among them. A broad sheet of flame went up from the corner of the roof immediately above Miss Parrish's room. With a hundred smaller flames flicking out from it in all directions, the section of roof sank slowly inwards in a seething mass of cinders, and then finally went down with a rush as that whole side of the top story collapsed with a fiery crash.

* * *

On the following morning, when the sun's earliest rays were not yet warm enough to dry the dew from the grass, a buckboard drove up to one of the houses on the slope of the hill and stopped, and a man with a large battered hat and a large grey moustache got down and looked about for somewhere to tie the team.

Mrs. Meade stood looking out of an upstairs window, clad in a black silk dress that did not fit her too well—a hasty loan from the neighbor who had opened her home to a portion of the Lansburys' guests; a lady whose name Mrs. Meade could not even remember. The black dress made her face, already a little paler than usual, look tired and older as she gazed down toward the mist-shrouded bend in the road beyond which the tragedy had taken place. But when the rattle of the approaching buckboard attracted her attention and she looked down to see the driver descend, she gave an inadvertent little exclamation and left the window to go downstairs and meet him.

Sheriff Andrew Royal was already in the hall when she reached it, his hat in his hand and his coarse grey hair looking a little more unkempt than usual, as if he had gotten out of bed to come. He cleared his throat twice in a businesslike way before speaking.

"I heard you were up here," he said gruffly, "so I came up to see if there was — anything I could (erhm!) do for you."

"That's very kind of you," said Mrs. Meade. She was more touched than she could very well express without terribly embarrassing the gruff sheriff. She had not expected it of him to come all this way just to see that she was all right.

There was a short pause. "It's all so dreadful," said Mrs. Meade. "That poor Miss Parrish — I can't help feeling there ought to have been *something* I could have done."

"That the woman who was killed?" said Royal. Mrs. Meade nodded. Andrew Royal gave a brief, decisive shake of the head. "Whoever's fault it was, it couldn't have been yours."

He inspected the brim of his hat, then cleared his throat grimly again. "You're sure there isn't anything I can do?"

"Well, as a matter of fact, there is," said Mrs. Meade, whose practical side never deserted her for long. "At the first alarm last night I threw my satchel out of the window. If you have a moment, you might go round back of where the house was and see if by any chance it escaped the flames. I felt—it would be rather insensitive to ask anyone connected with the house to do it."

Royal looked surprised, but acquiesced willingly enough. Perhaps he had not expected such a literal acceptance of his offer, but since his idea of "doing something" to help was very vague indeed, it may have been better for him that he was asked for a favor he could easily perform.

No sooner had he gone out than Mrs. Meade heard another familiar voice speaking in the entryway to the maid who answered the door, and a moment later Mrs. Lansbury came in. She, like Mrs. Meade, was attired in borrowed clothes, and the dark shadows under her eyes betrayed how dreadfully she had been tried over the past twelve hours.

She greeted Mrs. Meade quietly, with a quick clasp of her hand. "How are all of you here?" she asked.

"The others are still in bed," said Mrs. Meade. "Mrs. Grey's nerves are quite in pieces, and poor little Rose is just worn out."

"Then I had better not disturb them," said Mrs. Lansbury.

"And Mark?"

Mrs. Lansbury drew a slightly unsteady breath, but managed a smile. "He's fine. He was a little bit shaken up, so I've made him stay in bed too." She added in a lower tone, "I can only thank God it— wasn't worse."

She turned abruptly and walked across the room. "And yet how can I feel thankful for anything, or begin to regret anything — with Eloisa dead in this way. I feel I ought not to be able to even *think* of anything else."

"You mustn't blame yourself for that," said Mrs. Meade firmly.

Mrs. Lansbury shook her head. "It was in my home, it was I who asked her here; it was —" She paused, and bit her lip. "It was my responsibility."

After a few moments of silence, Mrs. Meade said, "Have you lost — everything?"

"Very nearly everything, yes," said Mrs. Lansbury with a sigh. "The men moved out a few pieces of furniture from downstairs, but the rest is gone. I caught up my little jewel-case on my way out of my room. But the earrings I wore last evening I'd laid down on my bureau instead of putting them in the case, so they're gone too — and I feel such a fool for even thinking of them at all." She drew herself up a bit more resolutely. "The house doesn't matter so much. We're insured — rather well insured — so we won't suffer in the long run. It's only the family keepsakes and valuables that can't be replaced that one regrets."

She added, "Mr. Emery has been very kind and helpful. He's gone to telegraph to Denver for me...and he is going to attend to the funeral arrangements."

Before Mrs. Meade could reply, there was an explosion of sound in the entryway — loud footsteps and voices, and then Andrew Royal strode into the room, a somewhat singed carpetbag in his hand and his moustache bristling.

"If I had any patience," he said, "I wouldn't spend it on a stiff-backed, mule-headed windbag like this one! Where's his right, I'd like to know!"

"Why, Andrew! Is something the matter?" said

Mrs. Meade.

Royal huffed with immense scorn. "I'll say there is. I went round to look for your bag like you asked, and I found it, stuck in a bush outside of the ashes. Just as I was pulling it out, a fellow pops up from nowhere and asks me what I think I'm doing. I tell him it's none of his business" (Mrs. Meade could picture this exchange quite vividly) "but I'm taking the bag to the lady it belongs to. This fellow doesn't believe me and says he won't let me off with it till he does. And he announces his intentions to stick to me like Missouri mud until it gets proved to him that it *does* belong to a lady, and that the lady exists at all!" Royal came to a stop, hot, red, and out of breath.

"But who was he?" said Mrs. Lansbury. "This sounds extraordinary. What was he doing around our house—and why should he be so concerned about the bag?"

"He's out there," said Sheriff Royal, jerking a thumb over his shoulder toward the entry. "Had to bring him up here—only way I could shake him off, short of arresting him. Here, you—get in here!"

He stomped back through the door and prodded into the ladies' presence, much to their astonishment, the dignified butler who had waited upon the Lansburys' table at dinner the evening before.

The butler was a broad-shouldered, heavily-built man of no great height, with short-cropped hair thinning on the top of his head. At the moment he was a shade less dignified than usual, bearing a suspicious spark in his eye and the general air of simmering wrath that most people exhibited following a dispute with Andrew Royal.

"Why, Chalmers!" said Mrs. Lansbury, too

surprised to think of anything else to say.

"Yes, ma'am," said (or rather retorted) Chalmers.

Sheriff Royal pointed at Mrs. Meade. "You see this lady?"

Chalmers nodded.

"You recognize her?"

Another short nod. "A guest at the Lansburys'."

"This is Mrs. Lansbury," Mrs. Meade interposed for Royal's benefit, with an indicative gesture.

The sheriff nodded. "Right. And this is the lady that belongs to this bag. D'you recognize the bag, Mrs. Meade?"

"Yes, that is mine."

"It's yours?" said Chalmers rather suspiciously.

"Certainly."

"Satisfied?" demanded Royal.

Chalmers looked slightly disgruntled, but indicated that he was.

He turned and addressed Mrs. Lansbury. "I beg pardon for causing a commotion, ma'am. But when I see a strange gentleman removing a bag from your premises in a suspicious manner, I'm naturally bound to see that there's nothing wrong about it, aren't I?"

"Yes—quite naturally, Chalmers," said Mrs. Lansbury rather faintly. "You may go now."

Chalmers bowed with all his accustomed dignity and withdrew, without a glance for Sheriff Royal (who had nearly had an apoplectic fit at the words "a suspicious manner").

When the front door had closed, betokening that the butler was definitely out of earshot, the sheriff exploded. "Natural my foot! I'll be keeping my eye on that fellow, I can tell you that!" He appeared to recollect the presence of the carpetbag in his hand for the first time, and thumped it down on the seat of a nearby chair. "If you ask me, *he's* the most likely one to suspect."

"Suspect! Suspect him of what?" said Mrs. Meade.

"Good Lord, what do you suppose I'm here for?" said Andrew Royal crossly.

Mrs. Meade heard a quick intake of breath before Mrs. Lansbury spoke. "Do you mean that there is something—"

Royal, who abhorred anything like a "scene," interrupted her brusquely, determined to diffuse any vestige of suspense or drama that might lead to such. "A couple of the men who helped fight that fire saw some things that struck them as funny. They talked it over and decided to call me in to take a look at it."

A chill ran through Mrs. Meade. "They think the fire was deliberately set?"

Royal spoke brusquely. "When there's bonfires built up in the corners of a room made out of the books off the shelves and the cushions off the sofas, it doesn't exactly look like an accident."

* * *

Sheriff Andrew Royal never wasted any time in getting down to business once fairly launched on an investigation. He attacked any possible witnesses with a promptitude and efficiency that frequently left them gasping as if a tornado had hit them. In consequence of this, shortly after noon Mrs. Meade received a frantic summons upstairs to the bedroom from which Mrs. Grey had not yet emerged, and guessed quite accurately the reason why.

Mrs. Grey was in bed still, half propped up against the pillows, with nervous eyes and anxiously drawn forehead and hands that could not keep still upon the coverlet. When she saw Mrs. Meade she stretched out a hand to her in a distressed way, and Mrs. Meade took it reassuringly in both of her own as she sat down on the edge of the bed. Rose, who had brought Mrs. Meade the message from her mother, closed the bedroom door and came to stand by the foot with her arm linked around the bedpost.

"Letitia, what on earth is going *on*?" implored Mrs. Grey. "There was a sheriff up here a little while ago, and he was asking us all sorts of questions about the fire — where we were when it started, and who we saw, and — everything. What does he mean by it?"

"It isn't anything to do with you, really," said Mrs. Meade; "he is only questioning anyone who happened to be in the house."

"But why? What is it all about?"

Mrs. Meade hesitated just a little, choosing her words carefully in her desire to be truthful without distressing Mrs. Grey any further. Evasion was worth nothing, but she wished to make the affair sound as insignificant as possible. "He is only trying to discover just how the fire started. Some of the men who helped to fight it were puzzled by the way things looked downstairs, so the sheriff wants to clear the matter up directly."

She was looking at the other woman's face as she spoke, and saw that Mrs. Grey, in spite of her nerves, could still understand what this meant. A look of amazement momentarily overcame the fearfulness in her eyes. "Do you mean — they think the fire was not an accident?"

"From what I understand, yes."

"But—why would anyone want to *start* a fire?" said Rose.

"I don't know, dear. Let us just hope the sheriff will be able to find that out soon. At any rate, I don't think he will be troubling you again." Mrs. Meade gave her friend's hand another comforting pat before she released it and stood up. "If there is anything else you need, be sure to call me. I won't be far away."

"Yes—yes, of course," said Mrs. Grey, who seemed to be thinking of something else, her troubled eyes wandering about the room. "I will. Thank you very much, Letitia." She looked back up at Mrs. Meade and managed a tired smile.

Rose accompanied Mrs. Meade to the door and opened it for her. Mrs. Meade paused in the doorway, and looked back toward the bed.

"She's very upset."

"Yes," said Rose.

Mrs. Meade looked at her. Rose's answer had been simple agreement. The very slight inflection of questioning in Mrs. Meade's remark must have passed her unnoticed. Or perhaps it was a natural circumstance for Mrs. Grey to be very upset.

Mrs. Meade added in the same low tone, laying a hand on Rose's arm, "Don't you forget either, dear. I'll be on hand if you need me for anything."

Rose nodded, with a little bit of a smile, and closed the door.

Mrs. Meade went downstairs to the empty drawing-room and sat down. She thought back again over the events of the previous day and night. And the one thing that kept returning to her mind was the memory of Mark Lansbury's voice saying, "The essence of a man's character — the trial by fire, so to speak."

She sat still, while the breeze stirred the curtains and light gray clouds dimmed the afternoon outside. The drawing-room was shadowy by the time she heard a ring at the doorbell, and a moment later familiar clumping footsteps in the hall.

Royal came into the room in a way that indicated he had expected to find her here, for he made no initial remark or greeting as he looked at her. He scratched the back of his neck, and then sat down heavily in a chair opposite her.

"Well," he said, "I've got something. It's just a hint, but it's something. Might surprise you. And I don't think you'll like it any too well."

Mrs. Meade said quietly, "Is it something to do with Mark Lansbury?"

Royal's jaw actually dropped — he stared at her for a few seconds and blinked. Then he pulled himself together.

"You're right, as usual. Though I don't see how you can know it, unless you've already talked to the girl yourself?"

"Which girl?" said Mrs. Meade a little bit quickly.

"The maid. Mrs. Lansbury's maid. Seems she overheard him say something funny last night that put her mind onto it."

"When she — oh, yes. That would be it." Mrs. Meade nodded, reflectively. "*'It couldn't have been planned any better'* — that was it, wasn't it?"

"That's it. You were there too, weren't you? Now, what I want to know is *why*. The maid gave me a

long rigamarole about a romance and a rival and a rose
and I don't know what all, and I'm blamed if I can
make head or tail of it."

"That's very nearly it," said Mrs. Meade; and,
tailoring her narrative style to her audience, she gave
him, with as little sentiment as possible, a description
of the state of affairs between Mark Lansbury, Rose
Grey and Steven Emery.

Royal listened, and grunted without much
interest when she finished. "All nice for a novel," he
said. "But I don't see what it's got to do with the fire.
Still what the kid said sure makes it look like *he* had
something to do with it."

"You'd think appearances were even blacker
against him, I'm afraid, if you had heard what he was
saying to me yesterday afternoon," said Mrs. Meade,
"about how a man is only given a chance to prove himself in a 'trial by fire'."

Andrew Royal nearly jumped out of his chair.
"What!"

He listened much more intently as Mrs. Meade
explained the whole of the conversation she had had
with Mark in the garden. "So you think," he said, "that
he started the house on fire, so he could rescue the girl
or somebody, and make himself out to be a hero?"

"I should hate to think that!" said Mrs. Meade
with surprising energy. "It's only that I made up my
mind to be frank with you from the first, Andrew,
whatever my own opinions may be. I know it certainly
wouldn't do Mark any good if you were to hear of
such a thing later on."

The sheriff leaned forward in his chair,
examining her keenly from under his bushy eyebrows.
"Tell the truth, Lettie. You think the boy did it."

"I don't know, Andrew," said Mrs. Meade, looking down at her folded hands in her lap and shaking her head. "I've known Mark since he was a little boy, and I would not have thought him the kind to risk harming other people by doing something that could go so horribly, dangerously wrong. But he was terribly in love, and very wrought up over it, and he could have reached the point where he was ready to do something reckless."

Royal grunted again. "He'd have had to be pretty far gone. What kind of idiot sets his own house on fire?"

"Well, it's rather less audacious then setting someone else's house on fire," said Mrs. Meade. "If it comes to that, Mrs. Lansbury says the house was well insured. Mark likely would have known about that."

Andrew Royal plucked at his moustache for a moment. "Insured, eh?" he said. "Where's Lansbury Senior, now? His wife said he was suddenly called away on business yesterday."

"In Denver. But I don't believe he was called away; he told us all he'd decided to go himself."

"On the board of a railroad company, isn't he?" said Royal. "What's he up to just now?"

"I understand he's been planning the construction of a short new line to connect two busy existing ones—a rather bold project, I believe, since it will have to cross some mountains to do so."

"Mmm-hmm," said Royal. "I was talking to that Steven Emery fellow, too. He said Lansbury's having a job trying to raise the capital for it."

"Did Mr. Emery tell you why *he* had chosen not to invest in it?" inquired Mrs. Meade rather pointedly.

One corner of the sheriff's moustache bent

upwards. "I think Emery's a fellow who likes to put his investments in a basket he can be sure won't come back full of broken eggs."

"Mr. Lansbury is no charlatan," said Mrs. Meade, raising her eyebrows just a trifle.

"I'll wager he's no Rockefeller either. Could be he won't be too put out by his well-insured house's burning down just when cash on hand will come in handy."

"But he was not desperate," exclaimed Mrs. Meade. "The Lansburys may not be extremely rich, but they've been quite prosperous for—"

"For an awful short time. I'm not saying anything against your friend, now, but I say when money comes quick, you look around and see where it came from.

"Of course."

Sheriff Royal seemed more nettled by her unexpected acquiescence. "For all we know, all this could be built on borrowed money," he grumbled. "Three years ago Lansbury was just a station master, and now look—big new house, trips to Denver, son in college and wife wearing diamonds. And a butler. A *butler!*" repeated Royal with energy. "If you ask me he's the fishiest plank in the platform."

"I beg your pardon?" said Mrs. Meade, a trifle bewildered by the sudden change of attack.

"It wasn't natural the way he dug in his heels over that bag," insisted Royal. "Maybe he'd pitched something out a window himself—stealing, and started a fire to hide it."

"Burning down a whole house is taking a great deal of trouble to hide a theft," said Mrs. Meade, "besides leaving himself with nothing else to steal."

She considered for a moment. "Who gave the alarm when the fire started?"

Andrew Royal's face assumed a studious expression that was meant to be crafty. "What did *you* hear first?"

"I woke to a commotion and a voice somewhere in the house shouting 'Fire,' but I can't say anything about it other than that it was a man's voice."

"Well, there were only three men in the house — Emery, the butler and the kid. Want to know what they had to say about it?"

Mrs. Meade acknowledged her interest in the matter.

"The kid says he didn't wake up until a lot of other folks were already up and making noise. So whether he's telling the truth or not, he's no help. Mrs. Lansbury, now, she says that when she came out of her room Emery and the butler were both running around in the halls." (Mrs. Meade credited the sheriff with this description of the men's activities.) "Emery says he woke up to the butler shouting 'fire.' But this Chalmers fellow says *he* was woken up by a voice somewhere upstairs, and he can't even say whether it was a man's voice or a woman's."

"A man's or a woman's," repeated Mrs. Meade thoughtfully.

The sheriff threw up his hands and slumped back in his chair. "If you're going to look at it that way, there's only one person can be counted out."

"Who?"

"The Parrish woman. If she'd started the fire she'd have been the first one out of the house, instead of staying locked in her room."

"Unless it was suicide."

"Queer way to commit suicide. I don't think anybody'd have the nerve to sit and wait for a fire to come up to them."

Mrs. Meade gave an uncharacteristic shudder, and Andrew Royal at once looked two-thirds grim and one-third guilty. "Sorry, Lettie," he said. "I — er — forgot you were there. Er — " He cleared his throat several times and fell awkwardly silent.

Mrs. Meade had closed her eyes. She was trying to forget the image in her mind of a hallway weirdly lit in dull orange, the drifts of smoke clouding it, and an unresponsive oak door upon which she had beaten to no avail. If only someone had been able to do something...

Andrew Royal came out of his silence with explosive force. "I still think the butler's mixed up in it," he said. Mrs. Meade opened her eyes with a start.

Royal jerked a thumb over his shoulder as if the butler were somewhere outside the nearest window. "You saw the way he acted this morning. I'll bet he was hanging around there trying to make sure I didn't happen on any clues to how the fire started. Whether it was Lansbury or the kid who did it, he could've been covering for either of 'em. He probably thought the bag was evidence."

"I would hardly credit him with the feelings of a faithful family retainer, seeing that he has only been with the Lansburys for a year," said Mrs. Meade, drawing herself up deliberately into something like her former composure, "and before that he was headwaiter in the hotel at Coronet."

She frowned, hesitated and then spoke again. "But — if it *were* true — that Mr. Lansbury had arranged the fire — Chalmers could have been his accomplice.

Mr. Lansbury was away from home when the fire occurred, and Mr. Grey was with him to provide an alibi. Someone had to perform the actual details of setting the fire — Chalmers seems most likely."

"And what about the kid?" said Andrew Royal with unaccustomed shrewdness. "I'm not forgetting what the maid said he said. Suppose it was his father and *him* had the whole thing planned before he talked to you. He could have got to thinking the fire might do him some extra good in getting the girl's attention, too."

Mrs. Meade shook her head. "That doesn't seem quite right. I hardly think — "

"But the *butler*," said Royal, reverting to his pet theory without seeming to have heard her. He gestured slowly with a big forefinger, as if enumerating points of argument. "Suppose Lansbury was going to burn his *own* house — but wanted to save something — and he hid it *outside* before he left — " He stalled for a moment, still gesturing, but looking as if he had forgotten he was doing it. Mrs. Meade, perhaps for reasons of her own, forbore to interrupt his thoughts.

" — and the butler was *in* on it, and was supposed to fetch the stuff — and came around in the morning and found *me* lugging your bag out of the bush!" He sat back, looking rather exhausted, but pleased with himself.

She was not at all sure what she thought of this theory, but she did not altogether object to having the unfortunate butler absorb Royal's attention. So many things seemed to have gotten disquietingly complicated, and she wanted time to think them through.

Sheriff Royal's thoughts were moving along very different lines, but at this point they evidently intersected with hers.

He launched himself out of his chair with a quickness belied by his rusty appearance. "Why, blast it!" he sputtered, "if that's so, then I've let that blame butler go right back to get what he *was* looking for! Blast," he repeated in disgust. "I knew I should have arrested him this morning."

* * *

Lansbury and Grey arrived home from Denver the next morning. They found their families established at the hotel in the nearby town of Coronet, where they had moved from their temporary quarters in the neighbors' homes. Mrs. Meade and Steven Emery were with them, but Sheriff Andrew Royal was not currently in evidence. He had begun the day by serving a search warrant on the indignant Chalmers, who had taken up residence in the staff quarters of the hotel, their hospitality having been extended to him by his friend and successor as headwaiter. Having accomplished nothing here beyond creating a disturbance that eventually made itself felt as far as the manager's office, Royal collected his young deputy, whom he had summoned from Sour Springs to help, and began digging around the ruins of the Lansbury house, where he was still engaged in searching. With the possible exception of Mrs. Meade, however, no one knew exactly what he was looking for.

Descending the hotel staircase that afternoon, Mrs. Meade met Mark Lansbury on his way up. He looked a little soberer than he had two days before, yet he did not appear as strongly affected by the events of those days as some of the others in the party.

"What's going on, Mrs. Meade?" he asked her. "Do *you* know? Mother and Dad don't seem to be saying what they're thinking, but I don't think they like the sheriff's being here. And Chalmers has asked for his time. He says he'd rather be a waiter and not be persecuted, whatever that means. What's the sheriff looking for, anyway?"

Instead of answering him, Mrs. Meade came straight to the point that had been troubling her. "Mark, what did you mean the other day by saying it would take a 'trial by fire' to prove yourself to Rose?"

Mark looked startled. He stared for just a second, and then a look a look of horrified under-standing crept into his wide brown eyes. "Is *that* what they think?"

Mrs. Meade looked gravely and steadily into his face. "What *did* you mean?"

A rush of hot color had flooded Mark's face, up to his forehead. "I don't know what I meant," he said. "I just—said it! I never thought—" He leaned against the wall as if for support, his hand gripping nervously at the stair-rail. "Does the sheriff really think that I did it?"

"He—has his suspicions," said Mrs. Meade as gently as she could. A pitying, yet still puzzled frown rested on her brow as she watched the boy.

"Does Rose know?" he said almost in a whisper.

"No, I think not. I don't believe Sheriff Royal shared any of his ideas when he questioned her."

Mark came forward off the wall with sudden anxious urgency. "Please don't tell her, Mrs. Meade! Keep her from knowing *anything* if you can help it. I'd—I'd be too ashamed for her to even imagine that about me."

"Why?" demanded Mrs. Meade unexpectedly. "If Rose is such a romantic girl, she might think it grand, you doing it for her sake."

"No, no," said Mark, shaking his head distractedly. "I don't want her to know. I couldn't bear it. Can't you keep it from her? And then if the sheriff finds out something else caused the fire, she'd never even have to know they ever thought that — about me."

"Very well," said Mrs. Meade, her kind heart relenting a little before the boy's distress. "I won't say anything to her."

Mark thanked her, stumbling over his words, and then went up the staircase at the rate of three stairs a stride, as if he were afraid someone was after him.

Mrs. Meade went slowly down the stairs and into the lobby, and walked out into the grounds of the hotel. She walked along a smooth, well-kept path until she came to a bench by the side of it, and sat down. How long ago it seemed since she had sat on another bench in the Lansburys' garden in such happiness and contentment, and watched the sun beginning to lower over the verdant valley. Two days — only two days ago.

She considered what Mark had begged of her just now. In a way, she could understand it. Leaving aside the tragedy that had occurred that night, what had happened to him during the fire was humiliating enough, especially compared to what might have been. Mrs. Meade's lips twitched with half-reluctant humor as she pictured the opportunity for drama as Mark might have pictured it. To have braved the perils of a burning house to carry a fainting Rose to safety — to be the first one she saw when her eyes opened; to care for her and comfort her — and perhaps to open her eyes to the devotion she had scorned, the devotion of a young man who would go through flames to save her...

Instead, he had arrived late on the scene, had failed to save Miss Parrish, had failed even to find Rose, and in the end he had been the one to be unceremoniously packed out of the burning house over his rival's shoulder—insult added to injury. Perhaps the sting would be worse if Rose were to think he had planned it himself and still had everything go so awfully awry.

But there was still something wrong with this image...

Mrs. Meade suddenly wondered why Mrs. Lansbury had said *"It was my responsibility."* Had she known about some plan of her husband's that endangered her guests? Or was she blaming herself for having taken her son's unhappy romance too lightly?

Mrs. Meade did not put much stock in Andrew Royal's suggestion that Mark had conspired with his father. Mark was far too transparent not to have betrayed some underlying agitation or anticipation connected with the plot beforehand. On the contrary, he had been consumed with Rose and Emery that whole evening, and had barely seemed to notice his father's existence. No, if Mark was responsible, he had acted alone.

But something just did not fit...

A step on the path roused Mrs. Meade from her meditations. She looked up to see Steven Emery approaching.

"Oh, good afternoon, Mr. Emery," she said.

"Good afternoon," said Emery, as he stopped by the bench. He indicated the seat with a gesture. "May I?"

Mrs. Meade acquiesced at once and he sat down. He also looked, she observed, as if he had been thinking over something that puzzled or concerned him. He looked at her for a moment as if he had a question he was weighing whether or not to ask her, and then he spoke.

"Mrs. Meade," he said, "I heard something this afternoon which frankly astonished me. Is it true that the sheriff suspects Mark Lansbury of having set fire to the house the other night?"

"How did you hear that?" said Mrs. Meade, her thoughts going at once to Rose.

"I went over to the site of the house this afternoon, to see if I might be of some use to the men who are salvaging what they can. Sheriff Royal and his deputy have been over there nearly all day searching for clues. As I was going up the walk, I heard the sheriff speaking in a loud voice somewhere just around the corner of the ruins. From what he said, I gathered — but I could hardly believe it." He added, "I also heard the sheriff mention your name, as if he had discussed it with you, so I wondered if you might be able to tell me something more."

"There isn't much more to tell, I'm afraid — beyond the fact that he is suspected."

"But on what grounds?"

"On the grounds of something overheard, curiously enough," said Mrs. Meade, and Steven Emery smiled a little as though accepting a reproof. "It was something one of the maids heard Mark say, in the midst of the confusion that night."

She seemed to hesitate, and then went on in a lower voice, as if sharing a confidence, "You see, Mr. Emery...Mark is at a rather difficult time, for him. He's an impetuous boy, and he wants to prove himself at something—anything. Only the other day he was telling me he wished for some opportunity, some 'trial by fire' to pass through so he could prove himself by it."

Emery looked amazed. "He said *that*?"

"Yes, I'm afraid he did."

"What an extraordinary coincidence," said Emery, slowly. "But Mrs. Meade, if he spoke that plainly—of course I wouldn't presume to dictate to you, but—don't you think that someone ought to be *told*?"

"Sheriff Royal knows all that there is to know," said Mrs. Meade simply.

"It's really too bad," said Steven Emery, shaking his head. He looked over at Mrs. Meade with a regretful half-smile. "I would have to be a very blind man indeed not to see that Mark regards me with less than friendly feelings, but I can't help liking him in spite of it. I suppose all we can hope is that they won't be too hard on him."

He stood up, and looked toward the hotel. "I had better be getting back," he said. "Thank you for telling me all of this."

"You're welcome," said Mrs. Meade. "And Mr. Emery—you won't...say anything about this just yet, will you?"

Their eyes met as she spoke, and Steven Emery looked as if he understood. "No," he said. "I won't speak of it to anyone."

When he had gone Mrs. Meade sat alone for a little longer. But the lengthening afternoon was growing cooler and she had brought no shawl, so presently she rose and went back to the hotel.

She met Andrew Royal on the last turn of the path. The sheriff had a streak of soot on the end of his nose, and sundry other smudges on his clothes in spite of evident efforts to brush them off. And from the way he eyed her, and waited a moment before speaking, she knew he had something to say which he suspected his listener would not like.

"No luck," he said at last. "I've dug round that heap of ashes and crawled through that garden all day. I've questioned that confounded butler until we're both black in the face, and I've even wired to Denver to check up on Lansbury's business. No leads. Now that Grey fellow, there's holes in *his* bank-book you could drop a caboose through, but that's no help."

He paused. "It all points to the kid, Lettie. I know how you feel about it. But where there's smoke, there's fire, and he's the only one with any smoke around him."

"I knew you would come to that conclusion," said Mrs. Meade, "and I understand why. But I've thought it all over very carefully myself, Andrew, and there are three things that do not fit."

"Such's what?"

"The books, first of all," said Mrs. Meade.

Royal looked blank. "What books?"

"You said the fires in the library were started with piles of books and sofa-cushions. Now, Mark has been fond of books his whole life. No one who is really a devoted reader would start a fire with books, if they could find something else handy.

"And then there was his shirt. I loosened his collar when he was unconscious, after Steven Emery brought him out of the house, and I saw that the whole thing was buttoned wrongly—all the buttons were in the wrong buttonholes. That looks like he had dressed hurriedly, at the alarm, rather than having been up before everyone else to start the fire."

"It wouldn't go in court," said Royal, shaking his head.

Mrs. Meade's voice suddenly grew firmer. "But that's not all, Andrew. There's one question I have been asking myself over and over: *Why doesn't Mark show remorse over the death of Miss Parrish?* We have been so concerned with the details, I think we've been in danger of forgetting at times that a woman died in that fire. *And that isn't like Mark.* If he really started that fire, and because of him a woman was killed, he ought to be absolutely sick with guilt. Why isn't he? He knows how she died. He was outside her door trying to save her when—"

Mrs. Meade suddenly stopped, leaving the sentence unfinished, her eyes fixed on some indefinable point in mid-air. There was a strange expression on her face. Her mouth opened slowly.

"Eh?" said Andrew Royal after a moment, when it was clear she was not going to speak again immediately.

"Yes—I see it all now," said Mrs. Meade in a hushed voice, without looking at him. "That was why it happened so quickly, when he was there in the hall. And that must mean..." Her voice trailed off. "Now I understand. And it's worse—even worse than what we imagined, Andrew."

Royal stared at her. Every sign of belligerence and impatience had left his weathered face, so impressed was he by the strange, serious way in which she spoke.

Mrs. Meade took a step toward him and spoke

in a low, hurried voice. "Andrew — will you do just one thing for me? Don't do anything more until tomorrow. Don't arrest or question anyone. It will only be a few hours' difference. There is just one thing I want to find out. But first — " She thought for a minute, and then finished with decision, "First I must speak to Rose."

* * *

She found Rose sitting alone in the window-seat of her hotel room in the near-twilight, her cheek resting on her hand, gazing pensively out into the softly gathering gloom. Rose turned slowly to look at Mrs. Meade as the older woman sat down opposite her, and Mrs. Meade saw that her gray eyes were dark and almost sad with thought, but in the shadowed corner of the window-seat her face seemed again very young and childish.

"My dear," Mrs. Meade began quietly, "there is something I would like to tell you. You may not understand it now, or understand why I am saying it, but I do not ask you to understand — only to take it to heart."

She smiled suddenly. "You are becoming a young woman, Rose, and I know you are looking forward to love. Every girl does. But it is important for you to always ask yourself whether a man's professed love for you is something that thinks only of itself — of himself. There are many people who can love selfishly, but that kind of love is not always the truest, even though sometimes it can appear splendid on the outside."

"You sound so serious!" said Rose, wide-eyed, her voice half alarm, half wondering.

"I *am* serious. But I am also sure that you will find a good man. For now, I only want you to remember—" Mrs. Meade hesitated. "Some young girls might think it romantic, a man committing a desperate act—a crime, even—for the sake of love. They might be flattered to think he had done it for their sake. But at heart it is only selfishness—a sacrifice of righteousness and honor so that he might have the thing he wanted."

She smiled again, a reassuring, motherly smile, and patted Rose's hand. "I think you will understand—some time—what I am trying to say. Will you only promise me you will remember it?"

"I'll try," said Rose faintly.

Mrs. Meade rose, and bent to kiss her cheek. "Thank you, my dear," she said. Then she moved quietly across the dim room to the door, went out and closed it behind her.

"And now," she said to herself, in the hall, "I must speak to the Lansburys."

* * *

The clock in the hotel lobby was chiming a quarter past twelve when Sheriff Andrew Royal labored up two flights of the broad red-carpeted staircase as if he were scaling a mountain, and looked about at the doors for the number of the room he was seeking. When he found it, he knocked, and in a few seconds the door was opened by Mr. Lansbury, who stepped aside for him to enter.

In spite of the lateness of the hour, there were three other people in the room—Mrs. Lansbury, Mrs. Meade, and George Grey. A lamp was burning on the table by which Mrs. Meade sat, and near it lay a small pile of papers and envelopes. The demeanor of everyone in the room, and the very silence with which they had awaited the coming of the sheriff, made it plain that something had happened, or was about to happen. It was also evident that both of the Lansburys already knew what it was, but Grey had not yet been informed, though from the look on his face as he waited he guessed that it was something serious.

"Thank you for coming up, Sheriff," said Lansbury, shaking his hand. "I have something here which I think you ought to know about. Mrs. Meade came to me earlier this evening and confided to me a theory she had about the cause of our fire, and asked my help in confirming it—and I think we may have done so." He glanced down at Mrs. Meade, and spoke to her in a slightly lower voice, tinged with a note of respect. "Would you like to explain it first?"

"It was something *you* said, in fact, Andrew, that gave me the illumination," said Mrs. Meade. "You remarked quite off-hand during our conversation earlier that 'where there's smoke, there's fire,' just as I was thinking over something that puzzled me about what happened in the upstairs hall that night. And suddenly it all flashed on me. I remember now that when I stepped out of my room that night there was already a good deal of smoke in the hallway. That did not seem strange to me, of course, because I knew there was a fire in the house. But now I recall clearly that when I turned and went along the hall to Miss Parrish's room—*away* from the top of the staircase, which led down to where the fire was—the smoke actually grew thicker. That was why I could not stay long by her door myself. And when I sent Mark up to try and help her, he was nearly suffocated up there in just a few minutes, while I, going down the stairs, found the smoke grew lighter as I went down and it was easier to breathe.

"Do you see what I mean? Where there is smoke, there must be fire. There was *another fire burning in Miss Parrish's room*, and it was from there that the smoke was seeping into the hall."

"You mean she *did* start it herself?" blurted Royal.

Mrs. Meade shook her head. "You recall my saying to you this afternoon," she said, "that the solution to this was something even worse than we had imagined. We have been regarding Miss Parrish's death as a tragic accident caused by someone's setting a fire for reasons of their own. But it was not. It was murder."

"Murder!" said Grey and Royal together.

"Yes. Do you know what I think? *Miss Parrish was dead before the fire had even started*. The fire was set expressly to hide the fact that she had been murdered — to destroy that part of the house so no one would ever know she had met her death in some other way. That also explains why her door was locked, and why she did not answer any attempts to wake her.

"I had guessed so far — but I still could not understand *why*. It all centered on Miss Parrish — Miss Parrish was the root of the entire mystery. Why Miss Parrish? What had Miss Parrish ever done that some-one wished to murder her?

"And do you know what the truth was? She had *married Steven Emery in California four years ago*."

Royal stared. So did Grey, for a moment, and then he looked up at Lansbury. "Is that true?" he said.

Lansbury nodded, and walked to the table, where he picked up one of the papers lying there. "Mrs. Meade came to us because she thought my wife might know the names of any people or places with which Miss Parrish had been connected in California. She had guessed at some connection between Emery and Miss Parrish out there, and we were able, by sending some wires, to confirm it. They *were* married, but he apparently left her about a year afterwards."

"Miss Parrish was a very proud woman, I think," said Mrs. Meade gently. "She resumed her maiden name when she came back to Colorado to avoid the humiliation of admitting to her friends here that she had had a husband who left her. It was a strange chance that brought them together here as guests in the same house.

"It explained, too, another thing that had puzzled me before — why Miss Parrish seemed to so dislike your Rose. I had put it down to mere resentment of another girl's youth and happiness, after the disappointment of the unhappy love affair Miss Parrish was reputed to have had. But really it was simple jealousy.

"I think Steven Emery seriously meant to marry Rose if she would accept him — but he was not free, and most likely knew his wife would never release him to marry another woman, out of her own resentment and jealousy. That was what made me guess at the relationship between them — what other reason would he have for wanting her out of the way? He went to her room that night — whether to make an appeal to her, or whether he had already plotted murder, I don't know. And he killed her. But he needed to hide the fact — not just the fact of his guilt, but the fact that a murder had been committed at all. For of course no one else in the house had any reason to murder Miss Parrish. He set a fire in her room and locked the door, to ensure that that part of the house would be completely destroyed. Then, to get everyone else out of the house and give his first fire time to burn, he went down and started the fires in the library and drawing-room. Then he roused the household. That was what woke Chalmers. In the confusion Mr. Emery even had an opportunity to make an apparent attempt to save Miss Parrish himself, which no doubt would disarm suspicion, and which he could make sure did not succeed. He *had* to go upstairs, in fact, to get Mark away from the door somehow before he succeeded in breaking into Miss Parrish's room, but the smoke in the hall had already done the work for him. So, with bitter irony, he ended up a hero for saving Mark."

"Emery," murmured Grey incredulously. He added half to himself, "And we'd have let Rose..."

"Yes," said Mrs. Meade, giving him a look of understanding. She turned to Lansbury again. "He found out, you know, that suspicion was attached to Mark, and came to me to find out more about it. When I told him about that unlucky 'trial by fire' remark of Mark's, he was amazed—and he said something that ought to have been very telling. He said it was a *coincidence*. From his point of view, it was! But if Mark really had started the fire it wouldn't have been a coincidence his saying that; it would have been directly connected. Mr. Emery was quite earnest in recommending that I repeat that remark to the sheriff, by the way, unaware that I had already done so! And if I'm not mistaken, when Sheriff Royal questioned him yesterday he even—hinted a few things"—Mrs. Meade was treading delicately here — "about other people who were in the house, to further cover his own tracks."

Mrs. Meade's lips tightened into a decisive line, and her voice became firm as it always did when she felt strongly about something. "It was a very bad, cold-blooded, *selfish* crime, for he not only committed murder, he endangered all our lives and destroyed his host's home while he was doing it."

Andrew Royal seemed to have a throat too dry for speech, but he made a gesture toward the table. Lansbury understood him, and handed over the sheaf of telegrams.

"But can any of this be proved?" said Grey.

"Well," said Lansbury, "all there really is against him is the fact of the marriage; all Mrs. Meade's deductions are still deductions only. Even Chalmers' testimony about the voice he heard upstairs won't count if he can't positively identify it. But if Emery believes he's safe — and if he is confronted abruptly with the whole story, just as Mrs. Meade has told it — he may give himself away."

Andrew Royal looked up from the papers in his hands, and his thick eyebrows were drawn so low in a threatening scowl that they appeared to meet in the middle. "He'd better," the sheriff said.

* * *

George Grey shut the door behind him, and stood a moment as if thinking something over. He glanced to his right and left. The hotel was silent at this hour, its corridors dim and empty. Grey moved away toward the staircase. Then a few paces short of it he paused, and turned to his left down another corridor.

He stopped at a door and rapped on it, a mere low knocking of knuckles on wood.

The door opened from within. Grey looked at Steven Emery for a moment, and then without invitation moved past him into the room. A single lamp was burning; curls of cigar smoke wreathed upwards above it from where Emery had been sitting by the table with a newspaper.

Steven Emery shut the door, his eyes following the other man as Grey took a short half-turn about the room, but he asked no question. He waited until Grey came to a stop.

Grey faced him, and looked him over again before he finally spoke. "They know everything," he said. "I've just heard it all."

Emery tilted his head inquiringly. "Who knows — what?" he said. "I don't understand you."

"They know that you killed the woman, and that she was your wife."

There was a pause. No reaction; at least none that Grey had expected. Steven Emery lowered his head slightly, as if giving thought to something. "Well, that alters things somewhat," he said.

Grey took a sharp step toward him, his frustration boiling up in his voice. "Why in heaven's name didn't you *tell* me?"

"It wasn't at all necessary," said Steven Emery. "Our agreement was straightforward: that I should loan you a substantial sum of money to cover certain of your defalcations" — Grey winced palpably — "and in return, you would give your consent to my marriage with your daughter. How I arranged my own affairs in order to meet my side of the agreement was entirely my problem to surmount."

"And you always intended to—surmount it in this fashion?" Grey's voice might have held a tinge of accusation, had he not been too conscious of his own doubtful position to dare it.

"I was not about to marry your daughter bigamously. My wife"—he pronounced the word with bitter amusement—"would not have let it pass unchallenged, and there was no question of a divorce." He bent a faintly amused look upon his companion. "You don't believe we met at the Lansburys' by chance, do you? I heard through your wife who Mrs. Lansbury's other guests were to be, and so exerted my considerable influence with your family and what I knew of the Lansburys to procure an invitation for myself. It merely saved my having to go in search of the lady." He added, "But I did not see the need to confide any of this in you."

He scrutinized Grey with a sort of curiosity. "For all your indignation, Grey, why did you come to warn me tonight?"

Grey averted his face with a vague wave of his hand brushing the question away. His voice was sharp. "Of course I would warn you."

Emery laughed. "Honor among thieves? Is that it?"

"This is no time for joking!" said Grey, coming back to him abruptly. "You have to leave here tonight. If you will turn over any assets you can lay your hands on at short notice to me—you know the other name and address—I'll send you the funds necessary for you to leave the country. It's the best way to keep all your property from being confiscated."

"And *you* certainly would not want that," said Steven Emery. "You'll do nearly anything for that money now, won't you? First your daughter — and now you'd make it the price of your silence and abet a murder. But I'm never one to refuse."

"You asked me for my daughter's hand," said Grey harshly, "and I laid conditions upon it. I was within my rights to do that, surely."

"Oh, surely. We understood each other's lack of scruples thoroughly enough by that time to make it practicable."

Grey bit his lip, and looked away. Emery, with a slightly contemptuous half-smile, turned away from him and took out a leather valise, which he began packing with a single change of clothes. New valise, and new clothes — like the others, he had lost all he had with him in the Lansbury fire. Sacrificed it all, Grey thought as he watched him. Calculated, unthinking destruction for gain, as Mrs. Meade had said. Well, there was one thing of his own that could be salvaged from the ruins — the good name and security which only Emery's money could preserve. Even at this price.

Grey said, "You do admit that my silence is valuable to you?"

Emery waited a minute before answering, without turning round. "Yes," he said.

Grey stood with his hand in his trousers pockets and watched him finish his packing, and nothing more was said until Emery had put on his hat and turned round with the valise in his hand. "Where can I communicate with you?" said Grey.

Steven Emery shook his head. "You won't," he said. "I'll communicate with you when I feel it's safe — and it will be at that other name and address you mentioned. It's in both our interest that you not let that become known, incidentally."

"You don't trust me," said Grey, "do you."

"Only just so far at a time," said Steven Emery, smiling slightly.

He stepped to the door and grasped the knob, and pulled it open. Grey, looking at the floor again, waited to hear him step out into the hall. But it did not happen. Realization of the silence struck him, and he looked up—past Emery, who stood transfixed in the doorway with his hand still on the knob, to where Sheriff Andrew Royal stood waiting in the hall, grimly silent, his craggy face thrown into grotesque shadow by the brim of his battered hat. Lansbury stood behind him. And Lansbury was looking not at Emery, but past him at his friend; and it was the disbelief in his eyes, more than anything else that was crowded into that moment, that at last made Grey look away.

* * *

"How did you know?" said Lansbury.

"I only guessed," said Mrs. Meade with a sigh. "It occurred to me, after we had established the connection between Mr. Emery and Miss Parrish... Sheriff Royal, you may as well know, was interested in the amount for which your house was insured against fire—he investigated your financial standing with the thought that perhaps the insurance money could have been useful to you just now. Of course he was wrong— but he did elicit the fact that Mr. *Grey* was in such difficulties. The burning of your house would not benefit the Greys—but if a wealthy man were to marry their daughter..." Mrs. Meade gave the slightly apologetic half-smile with which she was wont to deprecate her own accomplishments. "I thought perhaps it might be worthwhile to observe where he went this evening."

* * *

Mrs. Meade did not see Rose Grey again for nearly a month after the fire. At the end of that time Rose and her mother came to Sour Springs for the benefit of Mrs. Grey's health, her nerves having never quite recovered from the ordeal and what had followed. Rose seemed to have grown a little older in the intervening weeks, quieter and more observant, but her smile was still as quick and as sweet.

It was several days after their arrival before she and Mrs. Meade found themselves alone, sitting under the arbor behind the Colonial Hotel. A very light, soft breeze quivered the leaves of the clematis vines on the arbor, and the first fallen petals were already tumbling on the ground. Rose put out one hand and bent one of the woody tendrils of the vine, curling it around one of the slats of the arbor.

"How are you, my dear?" asked Mrs. Meade, breaking a short silence.

Rose looked over at her and smiled. "I'm all right," she said.

"You've been a very great comfort to your mother, I know," said Mrs. Meade.

"I didn't always *feel* like I could be a comfort to anyone," said Rose with a sigh. "It's all been so very strange—I didn't know where I was or what I was feeling half the time."

"It must have been very difficult for you."

"Well—I'm just glad that my father didn't know anything about the murder until afterward," said Rose. "It was bad enough finding out about the embezzlement, but that would have been so much worse. I've told Mother that, and I think she understands — although she's still terribly upset about it all."

There was a moment's silence. Rose looked down at the toe of her shoe as she smoothed out the short-cropped grass with it meditatively. "Mrs. Meade...could you tell me...do you think it's at all strange, if I don't feel — well, quite as upset as I ought to have been?"

"No," said Mrs. Meade, who understood the different inference in this. "It isn't a bit strange. I think it only means you didn't care quite as deeply, at the time, as you thought you did."

"I certainly never would have believed that then," said Rose, still staring thoughtfully at the ground.

Mrs. Meade quietly concealed a smile over her embroidery. "No, I think not."

"He was very — very handsome, and had such nice manners," said Rose with a little difficulty, as if trying to explain something. "He treated me like a lady — like a grown-up lady, and it was lovely. It was thrilling to talk to him in that way. But when I think about it now, I don't believe I ever really knew him, as well as I know — anyone else." She gave the older woman a quick, inquisitive sideways glance. "Do you think I still would have married him if he asked me — just feeling like that?"

"Good heavens, I don't know," said Mrs. Meade. "I only thank God you didn't get the chance to decide!"

"I did remember what you told me, and I understood," said Rose a little more quietly, "and it helped."

Again there was silence for a moment. Then she added, with a funny little tremble of laughter in her voice, "When you said all that to me, I thought you were warning me about — Mark!"

"About Mark!" said Mrs. Meade, letting her work drop into her lap as she looked up in astonishment.

"Yes."

"You knew that he was suspected, then?"

Rose nodded. "That day, at the hotel, I opened my door and Mrs. Lansbury's maid was whispering in the corridor with Mother's Nellie. They were saying how Mark must have done it — and I knew why. It made me feel so terrible. I didn't think Mark could act that way — it wasn't like him."

"It may not have stood up in court," said Mrs. Meade, smiling, "but that was what I told Sheriff Royal all along. As it turns out, you and I were both right about Mark. He would never do anything so thoughtless and dangerous, even if he does sometimes lament the shortage of dragons."

"Dragons?" said Rose, puzzled.

"I think Mark has yet to discover," said Mrs. Meade, "that 'dragons' are just another name for all the little ordinary difficulties that meet us every day of our lives."

"Oh," said Rose, perhaps not too enlightened, but looking thoughtful.

Mrs. Meade did not trouble herself to inquire why Rose had felt so badly over the idea of Mark's supposed guilt. But she was smiling a little to herself as she picked up her embroidery again.

ABOUT THE AUTHOR

Elisabeth Grace Foley has been an insatiable reader and eager history buff ever since she learned to read, has been scribbling stories ever since she learned to write, and now combines those loves in writing historical fiction. She has been nominated for the Western Fictioneers' Peacemaker Award, and her work has appeared online at *Rope and Wire* and *The Western Online*. When not reading or writing, she enjoys spending time outdoors, music, crocheting, and watching sports and old movies. She lives in upstate New York with her family and the world's best German Shepherd. Visit her online at

www.elisabethgracefoley.com

Made in the USA
Middletown, DE
13 April 2023